Hero Needed

Shay Lacy

CRIMSON
ROMANCE
Avon, Massachusetts

This edition published by
Crimson Romance
an imprint of F+W Media, Inc.
10151 Carver Road, Suite 200
Blue Ash, Ohio 45242

www.crimsonromance.com

ISBN 10: 1-4405-5691-1
ISBN 13: 978-1-4405-5691-3
eISBN 10: 1-4405-5692-X
eISBN 13: 978-1-4405-5692-0

Dedication

TO THE ACC LADIES WHO WERE MY FIRST SUPPORTERS. YOU CAN READ THIS ONE! TO THE WONDERFUL MEMBERS OF MVRWA, A CHAPTER THAT KNOWS THE TRUE MEANING OF SUPPORT. TO JILL, WHO TOLD ME SHE WAS PROUD OF ME FOR TRYING THROUGH THE DARK TIME. TO THE PANERA PRISON INMATES, WHO HELD ME ACCOUNTABLE. TO CONNIE AND JENNA, WHO HELD MY HANDS AND FACED ME TOWARD MY FUTURE. AND TO MY HUSBAND, WHO SHOWED ME OUR COUNTRY'S BEAUTY AND THE GRANDEUR OF WATKINS GLEN THROUGH A CAMERA LENS, AND WHO TAUGHT ME A NEW FORM OF COMPOSITION. HE SAID I SHOULD WRITE BECAUSE IT MAKES ME HAPPY.

ACKNOWLEDGMENTS

My thanks to the Watkins Glen Chamber of Commerce for the brochures that kept the information fresh in my mind, *www.watkinsglenchamber.com.*

CHAPTER 1

"I can't marry you."

Marisa Avalos felt tasered with stunned disbelief. She'd expected to finally set a date for the wedding and discuss details over lunch, not . . . this. She felt icy on the warm Indian summer day.

Denial came next. The rumble of an approaching train beyond the restaurant must have garbled Kevin Johansson's words. He looked the same as he had since high school—serious, chiseled face, short blonde hair, and intelligent brown eyes. He'd matured since then but he hadn't changed so much that he'd end their three-year engagement.

"Excuse me?" she choked out.

He sighed. "Marisa, don't make this any harder. I'm moving to California to join a friend's veterinary practice. I know you won't leave your mother, so I'm ending things between us."

Marisa's eyes burned as she fought tears of hurt and betrayal. Eight years she'd waited for Kevin, through college and veterinary school. And not once in all that time had he mentioned wanting to move to California. By concentrating on the train engine as it rounded the corner into view, she tried to quiet her roiling mind enough to respond coherently. Less than seven feet away on the other side of the restaurant's deck, the engine looked impossibly huge. The building shook, making the water glasses and silverware clink. The chaos of sound mimicked the chaos in her heart and mind.

As the engine passed, she glanced in the opposite direction, anything not to look at Kevin for a few moments. A hundred yards away where the promenade led up from the docks a group of people waited on the other side of the tracks. Her friend Carolyn Wentworth saw her and waved.

She nodded to her friend and focused on Kevin once more, sure now she could talk without crying. She had to speak loud over the noise. "But you're taking over old Dr. Handler's practice."

He shook his head and nearly yelled. "He likes working part-time. It could be another ten years until he completely retires and sells me the business. I want my own practice now. My friend from college offered me a partnership."

The shriek of metal on metal pierced the air from down the tracks, a sound that made Marisa's back teeth ache. The horn blast from this close was nearly deafening. As the engineer applied the brakes, the cars thudding into one another threatened to shake the building to pieces. Marisa feared a derailment. As far as she knew, there had never been a train accident in Watkins Glen. How much damage could a train going thirty miles per hour do?

Kevin must have shared her worries, for he grabbed her arm with bruising force and yanked her away from the edge. Other diners had the same idea, scurrying toward the side of the deck away from the train tracks. The wait staff hovered uncertainly, their eyes fixed on the train. Finally, the crashing and screeching ceased. The cars still swayed on the tracks. Customers murmured nervously. Diners from inside the restaurant spilled out onto the deck rushing for the rail. Marisa and Kevin pressed against the crowd trying to see.

A woman closest to the end of the deck screamed and other women echoed it.

One of the diners leaning far over the railing turned a white face to the rest. "It hit someone!"

A man's shout rose above the murmurs and gasps. "Call 911!"

"Jesus," a man swore.

The woman beside Marisa turned her face into the chest of the man with her. His arm circled her and he drew her out of the way. Marisa and Kevin took their places at the rail. Worry for her friend Carolyn's safety flitted through her mind but Marisa brushed it away. Caro was safe. A siren wailed from the direction of the fire station. Help would arrive soon. A second siren echoed from down the street at the sheriff's office.

The engine had stopped four cars away from them. The engineer knelt by the third car, where a white arm stuck out. When the man next to him rose, Marisa sucked in her breath in recognition. *No!* Her knees nearly buckled and she gripped the railing for support.

"I couldn't stop her. I didn't know she was going to do it!" Scott Wentworth's voice carried clearly. He wrung his hands in distress.

"Caro," Marisa moaned. No, it couldn't be! But she had to know for sure. She grabbed Kevin's arm. "That's Carolyn's husband. I need to get down there."

Kevin gripped her forearms and gently shook her. "Marisa, listen to me. If it's Carolyn, you don't want to see her."

"Yes, I do!"

She ripped herself from his grasp. Spinning around, she darted across the deck with Kevin shouting after her. A man reached for her as she passed a table, but she dodged his arm. Pushing her way past a knot of servers, she ran through the restaurant and down the sidewalk to the promenade. The train blocked the usual sight of boats floating at their docks on Seneca Lake. The autumn sun failed to warm the cold dread inside her.

Marisa paid little attention to the gawkers hanging over the deck rail as she darted down the lawn that skirted the train tracks. Some curious tourists had moved close enough to see the body, but she ignored them.

The gray-haired engineer turned at her approach and held up his hands to stop her. "You don't want to see this, miss."

She cut her gaze to Scott Wentworth. "Is it Carolyn?" She wanted him to deny it.

Scott looked pale under his tan. His immaculately cut brown hair was ruffled by a morning probably spent sailing on the lake. "I know she's been depressed over the miscarriage." His voice shook. "But I didn't think she'd do anything like this."

Marisa hadn't liked Scott, and she liked him even less for trashing Carolyn in public. If she killed herself . . . Marisa couldn't finish the thought because she couldn't believe Carolyn would ever do such a thing. It had been a horrible accident. It had to be.

"I want to see her," she told the engineer. He'd moved to block the body from view. "Carolyn was my best friend. We grew up together."

The engineer's face softened in sympathy. "You don't want to remember her like this."

"My fiancé . . . " Or was that ex-fiancé? She plunged onward. "He's a veterinarian. I've gone with him on house calls before."

He shook his head. "Nothing like this, miss."

The throb of the engine was a perfect counterpoint to the tension building inside her. Emotions welled up like an ocean breaker preparing to crash against the shore.

"Please."

She sensed him relenting before he moved slightly to the left. Stepping forward, at first she couldn't make sense of what she saw. The bloody, mangled mess couldn't be Caro. Marisa focused on the face. It was the same lean, plain face Marisa had seen all her life. Carolyn had been a gawky stick as a girl. As a woman, she passed for fashionably thin. Blood soaked her short sable hair. Marisa quickly jerked her gaze away, but it caught on Carolyn's right arm . . . or what was left of it.

The scene in front of her blurred. Horror threatened to tear its way out of her throat in the form of screams that would never end. But grief trapped them inside, constricting her breath. She wanted to fall on the body and clasp it to her chest, wailing for what she'd lost. She wanted to shout denials until they became truth.

She turned and stumbled away blind. Strong arms caught her.

"Are you going to faint?" a deep voice rumbled.

Words failed her, so she shook her head against a firm chest. Even the heat blasting from the still running locomotive couldn't warm her. She clasped her arms around her shivering body.

"Get a blanket," the man shouted off to her left. Then he said, "Where's the man who was with you?"

Marisa couldn't remember anything except the severed arm. There were people moving around her, people in uniforms, people with purpose. None of them seemed to be with her.

Then someone threw a blanket around her shoulders. She gripped the edges together and looked up at her Good Samaritan. He was a stranger she'd seen somewhere before. He had short hair the color of dark chocolate, straight dark slashes for eyebrows, and eyes almost as dark brown as hers. He had a jaw like granite and his white T-shirt clung to the shoulders of a football player. He didn't look like a tourist, but he wasn't dressed like the rescue workers gathering around Carolyn.

"She threw herself in front of the train. I couldn't stop her," Scott told sheriff's deputy Brian Nash.

Rage simmered just below the surface of Marisa's skin, not quite warming her icy chill. Could Scott shout it any louder?

"It was an accident," she murmured.

"Did you see it happen?" her rescuer asked.

She looked up into his stern face. His expression was serious, his intent dark eyes probing. There was a deadness in them that made her wonder what horrors he'd witnessed and where.

"No, I didn't see it happen." Part of her wished she had. She shivered again.

"Then how do you know it was an accident?" His tone was flat, but his narrowed eyes expressed his doubts.

"She waved to me just before it happened. Besides, Carolyn wouldn't kill herself."

"How well did you know the deceased?"

Deceased. Marisa shuddered. She'd never laugh with Caro again, never share secrets or dreams or hopes again. Never again would she experience the unquestioning acceptance she'd shared with her best friend. Her eyes filled but she tried not to cry. Her throat ached, and her chest felt tight.

"I grew up with her." Her voice sounded small and squeezed.

"I meant how well did you know her recently?"

Not as well as she'd wanted to. It was hard to spend time together when Caro lived in New York City. Long phone conversations just weren't the same as sitting on the front porch of the huge white house where Caro's family had lived.

"We talked on the phone as often as we could. She never said anything about . . . " she waved a hand toward the train " . . . anything like this."

"People often keep their true feelings inside, especially if they're dark feelings." There was no softening in his unsmiling face.

"Not Caro." Despite the tendency for her lower lip to tremble, her statement was firm.

"Nick," the deputy addressed her dark rescuer, "would you help me question witnesses, find out who saw what?"

"I'm not a cop, Brian."

"As a personal favor. I need all the help I can get."

Nick nodded, still unsmiling.

Brian looked at Marisa then. He had short brown hair with the ends bleached blonde by the sun. His tan uniform was crisply pressed, despite the noon heat. The crinkles at the sides of his eyes showed he laughed often, unlike his friend. Dimples framed his wide mouth. Despite his serious occupation, he'd been smiling every time Marisa had seen him before, except for now.

"Marisa Avalos, right?"

Marisa nodded.

"I know you were raised with Mrs. Wentworth. I'm sorry for your loss."

Marisa gulped back a sob. "Thank you. Deputy Nash, she didn't kill herself. She wouldn't."

There was sympathy in Brian's hazel eyes. "We like to think the best about the people we love."

Her hands clenched around the blanket edges. Why wouldn't anybody believe her?

"Ms. Avalos didn't see what happened," Nick told Brian. He frowned when he looked at Marisa.

She waved back toward the restaurant. "I was at the Seneca Harbor Station having lunch. I saw Caro standing at the crossing before the train engine blocked my view. She looked fine. She was fine."

"Marisa." Kevin caught up to her.

Her first urge was to throw herself into his arms for comfort, but then she remembered what they'd discussed in the restaurant. Kevin was leaving her. Tears welled in her eyes once more and her bottom lip trembled.

Kevin opened his arms and habit and a decade of friendship made her walk into them.

"You shouldn't have come down here."

"I had to see her." She thought he would have understood that after all the years they'd known each other. But she was finding they didn't know each other at all. She wondered whose fault that was.

"C'mon. I'll take you home."

She allowed Kevin to draw her away. The engine hissed, releasing steam at her retreating back. She didn't know how she was going to make it through the rest of the day now that she'd lost her two best friends.

*

Nick Stark watched the athletic blonde man escort Marisa toward the parking lot. They made a striking couple, completely opposite in looks. Marisa looked Latina, with bronzed skin and hair the color and sheen of black satin sheets. With her wide, full lips he assumed she smiled often. At the moment, she looked as serious as the blonde man at her side. Too bad she was taken. For a moment, when he'd held her feminine curves in his arms, he'd felt a stirring of interest he hadn't expected to find in his temporary exile to Watkins Glen. But he was doomed to be disappointed yet again.

"Nick?" Brian called.

Nick shook off the spell Marisa Avalos had weaved around him and approached the scene where Brian knelt next to the victim. Nick steeled himself for the gore. As an EMT with the New York City Fire Department, he should be used to seeing horrors. But he wasn't. Each scene represented someone's pain and someone's need for help. But this woman was beyond his aid. A familiar feeling of helplessness assaulted him. Here was one more senseless death to add to the dozens he'd seen in the past few months. What good was his medical training in a circumstance like this?

The victim was mangled, the scene bloody. He'd seen something similar at a New York City subway suicide. Sharp steel wheels were vicious to skin and bone alike. This poor woman, if she'd really chosen to kill herself, had gone through a lot under the locomotive. Nick hoped she'd died instantly from the impact.

"Yeah, Brian?" He and Nick had gone to college together in New York City and been close friends until Brian decided to give up big city crime and take a job with the sheriff's department in the tiny town of Watkins Glen, New York.

Brian signaled him lower and spoke so his voice didn't carry farther than the two of them. "Mrs. Wentworth is the closest thing Watkins Glen has to a first family. Her parents, the Easterlings, died in a car accident last year. She owns the salt plant. Well, now her husband Scott does." Brian's hazel eyes were thoughtful.

"Interesting. That's motive enough for murder."

"This isn't TV, Nick, it's real life. Step lightly around Wentworth. That plant is the town's main industry."

"What if he did it?"

"What if he didn't?"

"Three deaths in a short period of time, and now he's inherited everything. Seems mighty coincidental to me."

Brian gripped Nick's forearm. There was no hint of a smile now. "If the husband wanted his wife dead, I can think of a dozen sure ways to do it. None of them include coming to Watkins Glen to push her in front of a slow moving train. There's no way to make sure she'd die. We can't make accusations without proof."

"I saw her wave to her friend, Brian." Nick didn't know why he said it, but it had seemed proof enough to Marisa Avalos. "I was on the restaurant deck when it happened." He'd been calling 911 when Marisa rushed past him. He'd reached out to stop her, but she'd avoided him.

"She could have been waving good-bye. We need to get the witnesses interviewed." Brian handed Nick his spiral notebook and pen. "You'll need these."

Nick held back his quip about this not being the vacation Brian had promised him. The dead woman at his feet deserved more respect than that. Besides, this wasn't a vacation. He'd been forced to take leave to get away from situations just like this. He wondered what the department shrink would have to say about it.

Nick approached the deceased's husband. Brian might not approve, but Nick was curious what the husband had to say. The man was in his mid- to late-thirties and his clothes, although casual, were good quality. The man was doing well, being married into Watkins Glen's first family.

"Mr. Wentworth? I'm Nick Stark. I'm helping Deputy Nash interview witnesses. Would you mind taking me back to where the accident happened and walking me through what you saw?"

Wentworth rubbed his face. "Sure, but is this necessary? She killed herself."

"If your wife tripped, you'd want to know that."

Scott failed to hide a trace of impatience. "I saw her jump in front of the train. She'd been depressed the last few weeks, since the miscarriage."

Nick had lots of experience giving sympathy. "I'm sorry about your baby. How long ago did it happen?"

As they approached the engine, the blast of heat seared the

autumn air around them like an oven. Nick felt the rumble of the running locomotive through his tennis shoes.

"It was last month," Scott said. "Carolyn wanted that baby so badly. We'd been trying for two years."

Nick noted the wording of Wentworth's statement, that his *wife* had wanted the baby, not him. "Was this her first pregnancy?"

"Yes, and she took losing the baby very hard."

Nick knew about the psychological effect of miscarriage on a woman, especially multiple miscarriages, but could a woman become despondent after her first? He made a note on his pad about it.

"Had your wife been under a doctor's care?"

"Yes. She'd been treated for depression." Wentworth seemed eager to impart this bit of information.

"Was she taking medication?"

"Yes."

When Wentworth didn't expand on this answer, Nick probed, "Which one?"

Wentworth threw up his hands. "I don't know which one. Does it matter?" He sounded exasperated.

The man apparently hadn't been watching the national news where certain antidepressants were linked to an increased risk of suicide. "It might. I'll need the name of it and her doctor's name."

Scott stopped in his tracks and glared. "Why is that relevant? She's dead. She killed herself." He waved toward the train.

If she killed herself. Nick wrote down the shrink's name Wentworth provided. As they rounded the front of the engine and crossed the tracks, Nick saw blood traces on the metal. The scarlet showed up clearly on the tan and black locomotive.

He wished he didn't have to interview witnesses because he'd rather not be near an accident scene. It made him itch to get back to work where he could actually help people. But he was exiled from his job for another week and he owed Brian. So he and Scott Wentworth walked toward the promenade.

"You and your wife were coming from the lake?" he asked.

"Yes. We'd spent the morning sailing. I'd hoped being on the water would cheer her up. We could see the train approaching as we walked toward the tracks. She must have planned to kill herself then."

Nick was getting tired of Wentworth repeating those words as though the new widower thought Nick would forget. A woman was dead; he wasn't likely to forget.

They'd reached the brick promenade. "You stood where?" Nick asked.

Scott moved to the center of the walkway. "Here. Carolyn stood on my right and just slightly in front of me."

"Was there anyone else here? Or anyone behind you? Any other witnesses?"

"There were other people, but I didn't recognize anyone."

Nick jotted a note to ask around for witnesses. Civic-minded individuals would stay in the area to give their statements, but not everyone would want to get involved, especially if they were on vacation. And a lot of people vacationed here.

"How many witnesses were there? Were they men or women?"

"I don't know. I wasn't looking at them." Scott inhaled and added, "Four or five, maybe, both men and women."

Nick made another note to ask Marisa Avalos who she'd seen waiting with her friend. "Mr. Wentworth, I know it's painful, but would you describe what you saw."

Scott took a deep breath and breathed out. "The train was coming. We stood back a few feet from the tracks waiting. Then when the engine was almost in front of us, Carolyn threw herself in front of it. I grabbed for her, but couldn't catch her. I had to pull in my arms fast or I'd have been hurt, too."

"And did you see what happened to your wife?"

Scott frowned at him. "I told you, she jumped in front of the train."

Nick held on to his temper. "I meant did you see the train hit her?"

Scott shook his head. "No, I didn't watch her die. I couldn't bear to see that."

"I understand." Nick's gut told him Scott Wentworth had lied, but Nick wasn't sure about what.

CHAPTER 2

Nick couldn't find another witness to corroborate Wentworth's story. But he did find someone who told a different story.

The Voglers were a middle-aged couple who'd spent the morning boating like the Wentworths had. They lived thirty minutes away in Corning and kept their boat on Seneca Lake during the summer. They'd driven up to make the most of the sudden warm spell.

"The young woman dropped something," Aaron Vogler insisted. He had a striking black handlebar mustache.

"Did you see what it was?" Nick asked.

"No. I saw it flutter to the ground and the next thing I knew, she was reaching for it. I couldn't react fast enough." He gulped, his Adam's apple bobbing. "And then she fell."

"Did you see what it was, Mrs. Vogler?"

Peggy Vogler put her hand to her chest and shook her head. Her short brown hair was artfully streaked with blonde. "No. I was watching the train. All I saw was her arms outstretched as she leaned forward in front of the train. I couldn't watch the rest."

"Did she jump in front of the train?"

"Jump? No." Mr. Vogler shook his head. "Maybe she lost her balance, but I'd swear she wanted whatever she'd dropped."

"I just don't know." Mrs. Vogler looked distressed.

Nick thanked them and said the sheriff's department would be in touch if anything further were needed.

Why was Wentworth so sure his wife had jumped? Hadn't he seen her drop something? Until the train moved, Nick would have difficulty proving Mr. Vogler's version of events. He knew from his years as an EMT that people witnessing a traumatic event often gave conflicting stories. But why would a man say his wife had killed herself?

Unable to find anyone else who'd stood with the Wentworths on the promenade, Nick interviewed bystanders. Some had seen Carolyn Wentworth sucked under the train. One person had seen her fall, but that had been from fifty yards away and from an angle behind the Wentworths.

So Nick was left to wonder who was right: Scott Wentworth or the Voglers and Marisa Avalos? He'd like to help Marisa discover the truth.

*

"I'm sorry about Carolyn," Kevin said once they arrived at Marisa's apartment in the green and white Victorian up the steep hill from the pier.

"I can't imagine not being able to talk to her again." It had been hard enough living in separate cities. Marisa caught back a sob as she led him out onto the second-floor smoking porch. She didn't want to be cooped up inside.

"Do you want me to drive you to your office so you can be with your mother? You probably don't want to be alone right now and, well, things are kind of awkward between us at the moment."

His reminder brought fresh pain. Her chest tightened. She didn't need to add more pain on top of what she was already feeling, but she had to know.

"How long have you been planning to move?"

"You know I've wanted my own practice since I got my vet's license. I never made any secret about that. And frankly, I miss the big city. Marisa, I can't stand it in this two-bit town anymore."

She'd worried he would change when he went off to college, but three years ago, he'd asked her to marry him. And when he'd graduated he'd come home to Watkins Glen. She'd thought he wanted a life with her in this little town. But she didn't really know what he wanted. She didn't understand him at all.

"You never said anything about wanting to live in a big city." Marisa tried to keep the accusation out of her voice.

"I liked living in Syracuse. I didn't realize how much until I came back home. There's nothing to do here, Marisa. My idea of dancing isn't moving to the sound of a jukebox at the bar. I thought I could fit back in because this is my home. I've tried really hard these past months, but I'm suffocating. I'm stagnating. I want out."

He walked to the outer wall and looked down the hill toward the lake. "I'm giving my two weeks' notice today."

Marisa sucked in her breath. This man she thought she knew well enough to marry was a complete stranger. He didn't share her values, didn't share her dreams. What had they shared beyond some lukewarm sex? Not a lot apparently.

"If I didn't own a business with my mother, what would you do?" she asked.

"It wouldn't make a difference, Marisa. You won't leave her or this town."

It hurt to learn Kevin had grown beyond her. He'd actually left her behind when he went off to college, but it had taken them eight years to figure it out. He'd left her in suspended animation, his ideal of a high school sweetheart. But that ideal hadn't survived the separation.

She slipped the diamond solitaire off her left hand and held it out to him.

Kevin hesitated, and then took it. "I'm sorry to do this to you today."

"It won't be any easier if we wait. I'll box up your stuff and leave it at your apartment with your key in the next few days. I'll come by while you're at work."

"I'll leave your stuff by the door. Marisa, I . . . "

She held up a hand to stop him from destroying any more of her illusions. If anything else had been a delusion, she'd rather not know. "I hope you'll be happy in California."

"Thanks, Marisa. Are you sure you don't want me to drive you to work?"

"No. I need to pull myself together before I tell Mamá about Carolyn."

He asked in a hesitant manner. "May I kiss you good-bye?"

She'd kept the home fires burning for eight years. Even now, when he couldn't hurt her any worse, she still loved him. "Sure, a good-bye kiss."

He took the few steps to her, the distance that had seemed insurmountable only moments before. Sliding his hand gently along her jaw, he lifted her face to his.

His lips were warm, firm and familiar, the kiss relatively chaste. It was over before it began. There was regret in his brown eyes. His hand lingered for a moment against her cheek, then dropped away.

"Good-bye, Marisa."

"Good-bye."

Long after Kevin's car pulled out of the driveway, severing him from her physically as well as emotionally, Marisa sat on the porch trying to absorb the Indian summer heat. She felt cold and wished she felt numb. As she tried to come to grips with Carolyn's death, tears tracked down her cheeks.

She couldn't get the graphic vision out of her mind. It hurt so much to remember Caro that way. Yet, having seen it firsthand was the only way she could accept that something so horrible had occurred. Things like that didn't happen to the people you loved.

When Carolyn's parents had died in an auto accident last year, Marisa had been able to accept that. Car accidents were common. A train accident was a surreal nightmare.

When this bout of weeping was done—she knew there'd be more—she headed down to her office on Franklin Street. The beautiful, handmade clothes of her mother's business, Designs of the Heart, gave Marisa's spirits a small boost. Her mother had sewn her clothes all her life. When Caro's parents had died last year and left her mother without a housekeeping job, Marisa had leased this office space and invited her mother to take up the unused portion in the front. It was a strange mix, but it worked for her and her mom. In fact, her mother had thrived as a shopkeeper.

Marisa wondered why she hadn't inherited her mother's creative genes. Surrounded by Seneca Lake and the gorgeous waterfalls and magnificent rock gorge of Watkins Glen, she should have had some artistic ability. But she loved numbers and was good at math. She was an accountant, what some people considered the most boring and dull profession on the planet. Doubt gripped her—had Kevin thought she was as dull as her job?

Her bare ring finger mocked her. Swallowing the lump in her throat at his desertion, Marisa opened the door to her office. The old-fashioned bell happily jingled her arrival. Anjelita Avalos looked up from the counter and smiled. She was slender from years of hard, manual work as the Easterlings' housekeeper. At forty-six, her brown skin had recently begun to show lines, but the beautiful Latina girl she'd been was still visible. Her mother's black hair was curlier than Marisa's, her skin darker, but they shared the same dark brown eyes. Marisa was pretty certain her father had been white, although her mother had never said.

"That was a long lunch, *mi hija*. Did you discuss the wedding? Did you finally set a date?" Anjelita still spoke with an accent even though she'd emigrated from Chile forty years ago. She addressed Marisa with the Spanish word for daughter.

Oh, God, this was going to be hard. "No, Mamá, we didn't." Marisa tugged her mother to the visitor chairs in her office.

As they sat, her mother scrutinized her face. "Tell me, *mi hija*."

"Mamá, there was an accident . . . "

Anjelita sucked in her breath. "Was Kevin hurt?"

"No, not Kevin. It was Carolyn. Mamá, I saw it happen. She was standing at the train crossing. The train was coming." Marisa's throat closed.

Anjelita crossed herself. Then she covered her mouth with her hand. Her eyes were huge, her skin pale brown.

Marisa cleared her throat. "She's dead. It was awful. And her husband says she threw herself in front of the train."

"*Madre de Dios.* Not suicide!"

"No, Caro wouldn't do that. I know her."

Her mother looked away. "The Easterlings were not the kind to take that way out." She sighed. "She was the last. I did not expect it in my lifetime."

What an odd thing to say. But Anjelita had been part of the Easterling household for more than a quarter century.

"I'm not going to let Scott Wentworth get away with saying those things about Caro. I knew her longer than he did. She didn't suffer from depression. There has to be a way to prove she didn't kill herself."

"You do not know all that goes on between a man and a woman, *mi hija*. You and Kevin have not lived together. It can be hard on a woman to wait for her man to come to her after a long day at work. We do not know how Carolyn filled her days."

Marisa was distracted from her mother's intriguing view of relationships to defend Caro. "She didn't sit around moping, Mamá. She did charity work."

"Still, volunteer work does not fill all a woman's hours. She should have had children to give her love to." Anjelita's gaze on Marisa stressed her point.

"Scott said Caro had had a miscarriage." Although the idea was unpalatable, Marisa repeated it.

Her mother sucked in her breath. "Was this true?"

"She never said anything to me about it, and we were as close as sisters."

Anjelita's gaze snapped to Marisa's, filled with pain. "Marisa, there is something I need to tell you . . . " Her mother stumbled to a halt, her hands spread wide as though in supplication.

Marisa decided there would never be a better time. "There's

something else. Mamá, Kevin called off our engagement."

"Called off?"

"He's moving to California. He doesn't want to marry me." The last words came out on a sob.

"Oh, *mi hija*." Anjelita rushed to take Marisa in her arms.

"I don't know if he ever loved me," Marisa sobbed.

Her mother stroked her back. "I think he loved you with a boy's love. Now that he is a man, well . . . "

"When did he change, Mamá? And why didn't he tell me? Why didn't I know he didn't feel the same?"

"You were both so young when he went away to school. You both had years apart to grow into a man and a woman."

Marisa shook her head, denying, "But I haven't changed."

"You have, but you cannot see it. You are a respectable business owner now. You are involved in town decisions. You have a home of your own."

Marisa wiped her eyes. "But I'm still the same person inside that I was at eighteen. I still want the same things I did back then—a man to stand beside me, to be a partner to me, to be part of this town, and to raise my children here."

Anjelita brushed curls back from Marisa's face. "You are still young, *mi hija*. Do not give up on your dreams yet. There is that handsome sheriff's deputy, Brian."

But Marisa's mind flew to Brian's dark friend. There was a man to dream about.

*

"What do you think of the friend's claim that it wasn't suicide?" Nick accepted the cold Diet Coke Brian handed him.

His friend swung into his desk chair. As Nick popped the tab and took a long swig, he leaned against Brian's desk at the sheriff's station.

Brian sipped for a moment. "I think it's grief and denial talking.

Marisa may have grown up with Carolyn Wentworth, but Mrs. Wentworth has lived away from Watkins Glen for several years. People change."

"And you think Mrs. Wentworth changed the fundamental aspects of her character in that time?"

"A miscarriage could cause depression."

"We only have the husband's word about that."

Brian raised one sandy eyebrow. "You don't believe him?"

"The man just inherited a salt plant and who knows how much money and property. I think the least you should do is investigate to make sure he didn't push her to speed up that inheritance."

Brian frowned. "You've grown cynical, Nick."

"Yeah. Living in New York City can do that to people."

"Maybe it's time you got away."

"I am away."

"I mean permanently."

"I'm an EMT. It's more than what I do. It's who I am." Nick wished the department shrink had understood that.

"You can be an EMT anywhere. Hell, you could do that here."

Nick tried to make a joke of it. "In podunk? What kind of emergencies do you have here? Dog bites?"

But Brian didn't play along. "Women falling in front of moving trains."

Nick frowned. "There is that."

"I'm serious, Nick. If the city's affecting you like that, it's time to look around and see where you can get back to the man you were in college. Like I did. Your leave is a wake-up call. Plenty of cities and towns need experienced EMTs."

Nick hedged, staring out the window at Franklin Street. "So many people in New York City need my help."

"People everywhere need your help. Think about where you'd go if you could live anywhere in the country. Like someplace warm, where they don't have New York winters. Or you could live in a ski town and learn to ski. There are plenty of fishing towns between here and Minnesota. You could pick someplace beautiful so you can take plenty of photographs in your spare time. Just think about it."

Spare time, ha. Lately Nick's whole life had been consumed by work. Hobbies and friends had taken a back seat to his obsession to save as many New Yorkers as he could. Because of that obsession, Nick now had the time to pursue friends and hobbies.

He'd like to pursue one dark-haired woman in Watkins Glen. "I'll think about it." He sat in the visitor's chair on the other side of Brian's desk. "Who was the blonde man with Marisa Avalos?"

"Her fiancé, Kevin Johansson. He's one of the town vets."

Fiancé. Too bad. Well that was to be expected with a woman as striking as Marisa.

"She's never dated anyone but Johansson," Brian continued. "They've been together since high school. Maybe in the face of today's tragedy, they'll finally get married."

"Tragedies tend to make you re-evaluate your life." Nick's father's death had done that to him. He'd decided if he couldn't save his father, he was going to try to save everyone else.

Brian leaned back in his chair. "It's good that Marisa has someone to comfort her. She's got to be devastated. She lived on the Easterling estate and her mother raised the two girls together."

"I thought you said Carolyn's mother was alive until last year?"

"She was paralyzed during Carolyn's birth. Afterwards she had only one functioning limb. That's why Mr. Easterling brought Marisa's mom in to be housekeeper. Of course, the town gossip says he brought her in to be his mistress too."

If Marisa's mother looked anything like her, Nick could see why a man might do that.

"The other rumor is that Mr. Easterling got Marisa's mom pregnant and moved her to the estate so she could be close to him."

Nick whistled. "If she's an Easterling, then Wentworth wouldn't have a motive to kill his wife."

But Brian shook his head. "I don't believe Easterling was her father. But I think their situation was ripe to create rumors. Everyone loves a scandal, especially in a small town.

"Speaking of rumors," Brian continued, "I think Scott and Carolyn Wentworth had a prenup."

Nick sat up straighter. "Can you find out for sure?"

"Yep." Brian tapped his index finger to his lips in thought. "It'd be interesting to see if it contained a death clause."

CHAPTER 3

"I want an autopsy on Carolyn Wentworth," Marisa said the next morning at the sheriff's office. Finding only Brian's dark friend present took some of the wind out of her sails.

He rose from his chair and answered in a deep baritone. "An autopsy is standard procedure in possible suicides."

Well that deflated her righteous anger. She tried not to stare at him . . . what was his name? But he was compelling to look at in his tight, faded jeans and his navy NYFD T-shirt that stretched over a muscular chest. His intensity was palpable. She couldn't look away.

He held out a hand to her. "I'm Nick Stark. You probably don't remember my name. You were pretty distressed."

"You're right. I'm sorry. Are you a policeman?" She shook his hand. It was strong and warm.

"I'm an EMT with the New York City Fire Department. I'm on vacation." Some dark tone colored his words.

She frowned. "What are you doing at the sheriff's office?"

Nick grimaced. "They're short-handed, so I'm watching the phones as a personal favor to Brian."

"I'm sure the sheriff's department appreciates your help. As a Watkins Glen business owner, I'd like to say thank you."

"It feels good to be needed, even if it's to answer phones." Again, there was a bitter quality to his words.

"How long until we know the result of Caro's autopsy?"

"Your friend's body was transported yesterday to Montour Falls Hospital. That's the closest coroner. The coroner said he'd try to get to the autopsy later this morning."

Only a few more hours and she'd know. Marisa swallowed.

"Would you ask Deputy Nash to ask the coroner to check if Caro had been pregnant?"

Nick lifted one dark eyebrow. "You don't believe her husband's story?"

"No, I don't. Caro would have told me."

"Interesting. Mr. Wentworth didn't want an autopsy. He claimed his wife had been through enough already."

Marisa's heart rate speeded up with excitement. She was sure an autopsy would provide answers. It would prove that Caro's death had been an accident and shut jackass Scott's foul mouth.

Imagine him pretending he cared about Caro. He'd been from a good family and married well as both sets of parents expected. But Marisa didn't think their marriage was more than the merging of two dynasties. It certainly wasn't the dream marriage the 23-year-old Caro had thought she was getting with the dashing man ten years her senior. She hadn't told Marisa so much in words. Rather, it was what she left unsaid that led Marisa to believe Caro's marriage wasn't paradise.

If the autopsy made Scott look like a fool, so be it. But she didn't want to tarnish Caro by airing her suspicions about their marriage.

Instead, she said, "Scott probably said that about the autopsy because he was still in shock."

"You've recovered."

Marisa lifted her chin. "I need to clear Caro's name. That's the most important thing I have to do right now."

"What will you do if the autopsy is inconclusive? The train did a lot of damage."

A vision of Caro's severed arm infected Marisa's mind. Her stomach twisted, making breakfast sit uneasily. "Then I'll look for answers someplace else."

Nick drew a clean piece of paper to him, scribbled a note and rested his pen against it. "What number can Brian reach you at when he gets the results?"

Marisa gave him her business card. "Please tell Brian I'll appreciate the call."

There was an awkward moment when their business was concluded. Her mother's words about dreams and Marisa's response echoed in her head. And the shame she'd felt afterward for thinking of any man so soon. Nick Stark was only visiting Watkins Glen. Soon he'd be gone, like her fiancé.

"Good-bye."

Marisa headed for the door, but before she could reach the handle, it opened inward and Brian Nash entered. He was the antithesis of Nick, light coloring where Nick was dark, open and friendly face where Nick's was closed and stern, a quick grin instead of brooding intensity.

"Hi, Marisa." With his boy-next-door looks, he was a lot like Kevin. Unlike Kevin, Brian had no problem leaving the big city behind.

"Hello, deputy." She opened her mouth to give him the message she'd given Nick.

His jovial smile smoothed to seriousness. "I heard about you and Kevin. I'm sorry."

Yesterday she'd been inundated with condolences on Caro's death. No one had said a word about her broken engagement, although by mid-afternoon people must have known. Today that unspoken ban must have lifted. She wasn't prepared for the pain she felt. "Thank you."

"I guess yesterday was hard on you."

She swallowed before answering. "Yes."

"Let me know if you need someone to talk to. I can recommend some excellent counselors and you wouldn't have to worry about everyone in town knowing your business."

"Oh. Thanks, I'll do that." As she hurried through the door, Nick watched her with silent, intense interest.

She was used to being the focus of small town gossip. She'd be the hot topic until the next juicy morsel came along. Then her fifteen minutes of fame would end. She wished the hurt would only last that long.

*

Nick's glance speared Brian. "What happened between her and her fiancé?"

"He dumped her yesterday, while her friend was being killed." Brian's mouth twisted in distaste.

"Ouch. Talk about bad timing." Yeah, now she was available but grieving. Nick would be the worst lowlife to make a move on her now. He handed Brian the phone messages he'd taken along with Marisa's card with the note attached.

"Johansson's moving to California to become partners with a college buddy. Marisa didn't date anyone else the whole time he was in college. What a lousy reward for her loyalty." Brian leafed through the phone messages.

"Bastard." Nick felt like taking a fist to Kevin's face. Marisa Avalos was too good a woman to be treated like that. He was startled to think he'd based her character assessment on the fact she cared about her dead friend.

Brian poured a cup of coffee and sat at his desk. "Did a copy of the Wentworth's prenup come in while I was gone?"

"Yep." Nick gave Brian a smug smile. He searched through the papers on the desktop. "I read it. It contains a death clause. If his wife predeceases him, Scott Wentworth inherits all her worldly goods." He handed it to Brian.

Brian scanned it and whistled. "And her parents'. Very generous. But I still don't think he killed her."

Nick put his feet up on the desk and settled in. "You gotta admit it's a powerful motive. If he divorced her, he'd only get what he brought into the marriage."

"Scott Wentworth came from a wealthy family. He didn't need her money. I think she killed herself."

Nick frowned, tapping his fist against his chin. "If she was serious about killing herself, why risk a slow moving train? She could just as easily have been paralyzed or turned into a vegetable after a head injury. I would think having lived with a paralyzed mother that would be the last thing she'd be willing to risk."

Brian sipped his coffee before setting it down. "If she was depressed, she might not have been thinking clearly. She saw the train, thought how she could end her pain, and stepped out onto the tracks."

"But Scott Wentworth said they'd just come from boating. Why not simply throw herself overboard and drown?"

Brian lifted an eyebrow. "Because her husband would have saved her."

"You're sure?"

"I'm not sure about anything yet. You said the husband said she was on medication. Why not overdose?"

Nick nodded. "True. If she really wanted to die, why wait until she was in the town where she was born?"

"Maybe being here increased her sense of loss. Her parents are dead, so maybe that big old house haunted her. Maybe it made her depression worse."

"Yeah, and maybe seeing her friends with their children reminded her of the miscarriage."

"Marisa doesn't have children, and she was Carolyn's best friend."

She didn't have a fiancé now either, Nick added. Out loud he said, "You won't know anything for sure until you get the autopsy results." And maybe he'd offer to be the one to call Marisa so he'd get to talk to her again.

CHAPTER 4

"Can you come to my office at two?" Harlan Overmyer, the man who identified himself as the Easterlings' family attorney, asked Marisa later that morning.

She checked her Day Planner and saw she was available. "Yes, but may I ask what it regards?"

"Carolyn Wentworth's will. You're named in it and it's to be read today."

Marisa couldn't contain her shock. "But she's not even buried! Why the rush?"

"Scott Wentworth asked me to expedite the will."

Marisa bit down on the expletives she wanted to use against Caro's husband. "How can you proceed if you don't know the cause of death? The coroner hasn't finished the autopsy yet." Or maybe Nick had forgotten to pass on her message.

"Mr. Wentworth assured me the autopsy would be finished this morning and that the ruling would be suicide. I've contacted the coroner's office in Montour Falls so that I'll be notified of the results as soon as they're in."

Marisa ground her teeth together. All this haste was at the least unseemly. "I'll be there at two, Mr. Overmyer."

When she hung up, her mother called to her from across the room where she was stitching one of her designs. "What is wrong, *mi hija*?"

Marisa told her, unable to keep the bitterness from her voice. "He was married to her for four years. He's not spending any time grieving, but finding out how rich he's going to be. It's so cold and callous."

"Maybe that is his way of dealing with grief." Her mother's disapproving expression said she believed otherwise.

Marisa loved her mother for not making her hurt worse about

Caro's death, for not spilling additional poison into an already unbearable situation.

"Maybe it is."

"Marisa, about Carolyn . . . "

The bell over the door chimed and two college-aged women walked through. They made a beeline for one rack containing needlepoint blouses, exclaiming in delight as they held the first blouse up to examine it. Anjelita rose to assist them.

The phone rang and Marisa lifted the receiver. "Glen Accounting."

"It's Nick Stark." Marisa felt fluttery with nerves at the sound of his deep voice. "Brian just got the coroner's report. Do you want me to come to your office or would you rather hear it over the phone?"

Marisa braced herself. Her stomach tightened into a hard knot. "Tell me."

"Cause of death was blunt force trauma. She died instantly . . . "

Her breath whooshed out. "Thank God."

"Whether it was suicide was inconclusive. However." Nick drew an audible breath. "Carolyn Wentworth had been pregnant, but no longer was. The coroner didn't believe she'd delivered a full-term baby."

"No." Marisa's eyes filled. Caro wouldn't keep something like that to herself. "It can't be true." But Caro hadn't said a word to her, her best friend.

Nick's voice gentled. "Dr. Hampstead has been a medical examiner for twenty years. The sheriff said he's very thorough."

Fat tears rolled down Marisa's cheeks, dripping onto the audit reports in front of her. She tried to blot the drops from the papers before the ink ran. "So you believe it's true, what her husband said?" She couldn't even say the words aloud.

Nick sighed. "The sheriff can't rule it out. Not now."

"Caro wasn't like that. She wouldn't have killed herself." Nor would the Caro Marisa had known have kept a pregnancy secret. She'd have called Marisa to share her joy. The world was off kilter.

This was a bad dream and she'd wake up to find her friend alive and Kevin still her loyal fiancé.

"Your friend might have tripped. I'll ask Brian to do a little more digging and see what he can find."

Hope rose again, faint but breathing. "I'd appreciate that. Thanks for calling me."

"You're welcome. Marisa?"

She hesitated. What if he had more bad news? "Yes?"

"If you need someone to talk to . . . "

"Yes?" She held her breath.

"Don't hesitate to get those phone numbers from Brian."

Marisa didn't know what she'd expected, but his answer was a disappointment. What was wrong with her? Only yesterday, she'd been in love and engaged to be married. Now she wanted comfort from a dark stranger?

"I remember." She disconnected with a quick good-bye.

The world had gone mad. All of her anchors had snapped free and she felt lost and adrift. And then she remembered Caro's baby. Had the miscarriage sent Caro into a depression where she felt she couldn't talk to Marisa about something so personal and devastating? Had it made her not want to live?

Tears continued to run down Marisa's cheeks in ever-increasing numbers, destroying much of the spreadsheet. She found herself gulping sobs, and then loving arms were around her, her mother's familiar lemony scent in her nose. She clung to the anchor in this crazy world and cried for what she'd lost.

*

Scott Wentworth made a point to glance at his watch when Marisa arrived at the lawyer's office at five minutes before two that afternoon. Marisa wanted to hit him. Her eyes were still puffy from weeping; yet Scott looked completely unaffected by grief.

Even his hair was perfect.

"You cut that close," he said.

Marisa stiffened. She'd never liked Scott. Apparently, now that Carolyn was gone his animosity was out in the open. "Mr. Overmyer said two o'clock. It's not yet two."

Scott's face smoothed into an aloof mask and Marisa gave him a cold look. She didn't have to worry about strained relations between them because there wouldn't be any after Scott left town, and good riddance.

The inner door opened and a man who looked like an advertisement for the seven deadly sins appeared. His pate was balding, his jowls had jowls, his face was florid, and his expanding middle girth strained at his expensive charcoal gray suit. His blue eyes were sharp, assessing, as he took in the three people sitting in the hall. Marisa wondered who the other woman was and whether Carolyn had named her in the will. Perhaps she was a friend from New York City.

"Mr. Wentworth." The lawyer stuck out his hand.

Scott rose and shook it. "I hope you don't mind, but I've had my secretary drive down to help me clear matters. I'd like her to sit in on the reading so she can take notes." He waved to the other woman. "This is Brooke Shroyer."

The statuesque blonde rose and stood beside Scott to shake the lawyer's hand. As Marisa studied the model-perfect woman, her mouth nearly dropped open. How had Carolyn stood her husband working with this goddess every day? Brooke was five foot nine or ten, willowy, with the long blonde hair that drove men mad.

Marisa's thoughts careened to a screeching halt as Scott's words penetrated. She shot to her feet. "I object. This is a private meeting and Miss Shroyer isn't family . . . "

"Neither are you." Scott's voice was icy.

"Nor is she included in the will," Marisa said. "This is going to be stressful enough without strangers salivating over our distress." She included Scott even though she didn't think he felt any such thing.

Harlan Overmyer pulled himself to his full height—which was slightly less than Brooke's—and cleared his throat. "I have to agree with Miss Avalos. This is a private reading."

Scott's face flushed. Without a word, Brooke handed over a white legal pad to him. Marisa and Scott followed the lawyer into the tastefully appointed office. Being the Easterlings' lawyer must pay well.

Harlan sat in his leather chair, put on a pair of stylish reading glasses, and read the will. Carolyn left her parent's house and surrounding acreage and all its contents, and her portfolio of stocks and bonds to her husband. The seventy percent ownership in the salt plant went to him as well.

"I thought the Easterlings owned the plant outright." Was that outrage in Scott's voice?

"They did until a few years ago when they had to modernize. They sold off some shares to finance it instead of taking out a loan. Andrew Easterling always meant to buy the shares back."

"But thirty percent is a lot of shares. What if I want to sell the plant outright?"

Marisa gasped. Sell the plant?

"You'd have to put the motion before the board of directors for a vote, but you are the majority shareholder."

"I see." Scott wrote notes on his pad.

"The salt plant is our main industry," Marisa said. "It's always been locally owned."

"I don't need a salt plant."

Marisa's hands curled into fists. "You're a businessman and the salt plant is a business in the black. It's a good investment."

"Then I won't have any problem finding a buyer for it. I don't want to have to return to this place where my wife killed herself."

Marisa opened her mouth to utter denials.

"Miss Avalos." Harlan's carrying voice deflected their attention to him. "Mrs. Wentworth left you her parents' jewelry, including her mother and father's wedding rings . . . "

"What?" Scott sounded outraged.

"And the locket necklace her father gave her on her sixteenth birthday. It also says here there is a box of mementos in her father's office you're to have."

"Her mother's wedding ring was three karats," Scott objected. "It should stay in the family."

Harlan spoke in a soothing tone. "Carolyn was the last of the Easterlings. She can do as she wishes with her estate."

"I won't allow it."

"I've been custodian for the jewelry since Carolyn made her will last year. It's in a safe deposit box at the bank."

Scott's mouth snapped shut, but he glared at Marisa. What a miserly, mercenary man, begrudging some jewelry to someone else when he got millions from his dead wife. Marisa hadn't wanted the jewelry, especially the wedding rings, but she'd be damned now if she'd offer to let Scott have them. She could donate them to some charity in Caro's name, or sell them and use the money to do something for the town of Watkins Glen.

Overmyer closed the file. "That takes care of Mrs. Wentworth's will. Are there any questions?"

Scott spoke immediately. "I want to put the house up for sale as soon as possible. I'll remove any personal items first, and any furniture I wish to keep. I'll need to auction the rest. But I've got to be back in the city within the week for urgent business. Can you recommend a good realtor and auctioneer, and handle the details of the sale?"

Harlan laid his glasses aside. "Of course. But you might find, after a period of mourning, that you wish you'd kept the house. Maybe you should wait before selling it."

"But it's Carolyn's family home." Marisa felt sick at the thought of strangers living in the big white house. "She wouldn't want you to sell it."

"My wife is dead, Marisa. She has no use for the house now, and I live in New York City. The house means nothing to me, and the town even less. I only came here because Carolyn wanted to. My life with my wife was in the city, not here. Besides, I told you I never intend to return to this place again. It has the stink of death to it. Everywhere I go I'm reminded that my wife killed herself in front of me."

Marisa felt like she'd been slapped. Scott planned to systematically sell off everything Carolyn's family had accumulated over the past three generations until all that was left of his wife were the memories. This was awful. She was glad Carolyn wasn't there to see her husband's true colors.

"Do you wish to make the funeral arrangements or do you want me to?" the lawyer asked.

"I'll need to transport my wife's body to the city for the funeral and burial."

Marisa leapt to her feet. "No! You can't do that!"

"I live in New York City. My wife lived there with me. Our friends and my business associates are there. I want the service there so that the people who were part of Carolyn's married life can show their respects."

"But she lived her for twenty-three years. Most of the people in town knew her. We want to pay our respects."

"Perhaps two services," Harlan said.

"I told you how important it is for me to return home by the end of the week. I've lost my wife. I don't want to lose my business too. I've got to go through the house and papers so it can be sold. I really don't have time for a service here."

Marisa's patience evaporated. "You don't have to attend. I'll receive the mourners. But we deserve a viewing here. The people of this town are entitled to a chance to say good-bye." She refused to beg the bastard and she hated that he held all the power because he was Carolyn's husband. "I'll make all the arrangements."

"Fine."

Marisa had the feeling he'd gotten what he'd wanted. But so

had she. Now she had to plan a wake.

She took a big breath and braced herself. "When can I pick up the mementos Carolyn left me?"

"I'll have to find them first. I'll call you when I do."

She'd be lucky if he called before the end of the week. Just to make sure he did call, she pulled out a business card and wrote her home and cell phone numbers on the back.

"Here's where you can reach me." She handed the card to him.

Without glancing at it, Scott tucked it in his pocket.

"May I have your cell phone number so I can contact you?"

Scott looked mulish, but then he glanced at the lawyer and smoothed his expression. "Of course." He pulled a business card from his wallet and did as she'd done.

But as he held the card out to her, he kept hold of it. "This is my business mobile. Please don't call to chat."

Marisa snatched the card from him. Like she wanted to chat with him.

"And don't share that number with anyone."

She disliked Scott intensely at that moment. Had he been like this to Caro? Marisa hoped not. She hoped it was Scott's grief making him a bastard.

Harlan walked Scott to the door. "I'll call you when I secure a realtor."

Marisa's chest tightened. She wondered how her mother was going to take this news.

No sooner had the door closed behind Harlan, leaving Marisa, Scott, and his secretary in the waiting room, when Scott turned to Marisa.

"It's your fault my wife killed herself."

Marisa stumbled backwards at the unexpected attack.

"Because of you, my wife didn't make friends in New York City. You had to keep calling her and keeping her tied to this godforsaken town. No wonder she felt so isolated after the miscarriage.

"This past year had been hell on her, but she had no one to help her through it. Your calls were all joy and sunshine because your fiancé was home and all you were interested in was the wedding. What about Carolyn's pain? Her parents were dead. She couldn't even tell you about the baby because you wouldn't shut up long enough to listen to her. Some friend you were. You drove her to kill herself." He looked down his nose at her, his expression one of pure hatred.

Marisa couldn't breathe. She clutched her chest. "No." The word slipped out on a whisper of sound. No one had ever said such cruel things to her.

"You don't deserve anything from my wife." Scott sneered at her. "Now you know how I really feel about you. I blame you."

He and his secretary marched to the door. Marisa couldn't move. With his hand on the knob, he halted and turned his head. His cold eyes speared her.

"Your mother will have to find a new place to live. The new owners won't want her living rent-free in the guesthouse."

CHAPTER 5

"Sell the house?" Marisa's mother exclaimed, her face paling. She sank into the desk chair bewildered with her fingers covering her lips.

"Scott has no emotional ties to it, Mamá, not like Caro did."

Anjelita turned stunned brown eyes to her daughter. Marisa sat beside her and took her mother's rough, cool hands between her own, chafing them to warm them. She'd had to sit in the sun for an hour after Scott's venomous words to thaw the ice around her own heart.

"Then the Easterlings are truly gone." Her mother's voice quavered. "I never thought I would live to see strangers in that house." She opened her mouth as though to say more. Instead, she stared silently at Marisa.

"I know that house represents a huge slice of your life," Marisa tried to console her mother, "but it will still be there. I'm more worried about where you'll live."

"I can live anywhere, *mi hija*. But you have history there too."

Marisa swallowed through a tight throat. "I carry the memories in my heart, Mamá. I don't need the house in order to remember."

"He is a bad man to do this." Her mother's anger was all the more poignant for the tears that slipped down her cheeks.

Marisa thought so too. "We can't know how he's grieving about Carolyn's death." Wasn't that the truth? To say the awful things he'd said . . .

"A greedy man." Her mother sniffed and wiped away a tear with her palm.

Marisa sighed. She couldn't fight the truth. Wrapping her arms around her mother, she laid her cheek on the springy curls and inhaled the familiar lemon fragrance. Her mother was the only constant in her life right now. Marisa hugged her tight.

The bell over the door jangled. When Marisa looked up to greet a customer while Anjelita composed herself, she found Nick Stark standing there. Her breath caught. Her lower belly gave an odd clench. His dark intensity looked so out of place among her mother's brightly colored designs.

"I'll be with you in a moment." Anjelita dabbed her eyes with a tissue.

"He's not a customer, Mamá. I believe he's here to see me."

Nick looked just as serious as the other times Marisa had seen him. Did he never smile? That piercing dark gaze absorbed the scene, but his impassive stare gave nothing back.

"Mamá, this is Deputy Nash's friend Nick Stark. This is my mother, Anjelita Avalos."

Nick strode forward, a hawk among the tropical birds.

Her mother looked from Marisa to Nick with a questioning frown on her face. She shook Nick's proffered hand.

"Mrs. Avalos."

"It is Miss, or the young people would use Ms. I have never been married."

Nick's gaze pinned Marisa for a moment. Her breath backed up in her throat. He was so masculine this close she couldn't help but be aware of him. And she couldn't understand why she should be when just yesterday she was engaged to Kevin. Where was her loyalty to her fiancé? Where was her integrity?

"This shop wasn't here the last time I was in town," Nick said.

"We began leasing it last year," Marisa explained.

He looked around. "It's an interesting combination."

Marisa shrugged. "Neither Mamá nor I needed the whole space. Besides, it's a convenient partnership. We each help the other when we're not busy. Was there something you wanted?"

Again Nick pinned her with a look. Strangely, she felt stripped naked. "I thought you might need some breathing room from the townspeople. I wanted to walk the Gorge Trail and maybe take some photos. Would you like to come with me?"

Strange flutters invaded her belly. Be alone with this intense stranger? But after the visit to the lawyer, she really needed to walk off the stress and breathe untainted air.

Marisa glanced at her mother. Anjelita was frowning and Marisa wondered why.

"Mamá, do you need me to stay with you for a while?"

Anjelita shook her head. "No, *mi hija*. I think you need the glen. I know how much you love it."

"We'll have a special dinner tonight." Marisa kissed her mother's cheek and tasted salt.

"Be careful," Anjelita whispered. "Women can make mistakes when they are hurting." Her mother slid a significant glance toward Nick.

Marisa feared her mother could see the guilt written on her face. Was that why Marisa was attracted to Nick, because she'd been dumped? Well she wasn't pursuing any kind of relationship with him. She was simply going for a walk.

"I need to change into my casual clothes," she told Nick. "I keep a set here at the office. Would you care to have a seat and wait?"

"No problem."

*

As Marisa slipped into a back room, Nick noted her mother's stare was still on him. The woman had been crying when he'd entered the shop. He didn't know the cause, but he tried to ease her pain.

"The clothes in your shop look handmade."

Anjelita's chin came up. "They should. I made them." There was intense pride in her words.

"How long have you been making clothes?"

"Since Marisa was born."

"Where was your shop located before?"

"I did not have a shop. I was the Easterlings' housekeeper until they died. Then I had no work and there were no other housekeeping jobs in town. I am not too proud to clean houses—it is good, honest work—but Marisa knew I would be much happier tending my own shop. I love to sew beautiful clothes. She is a good daughter. She leased this place so I would be able to earn my living doing what I love."

So it wasn't just her friend that Marisa treated well. He'd been right about her character. "That was a very nice thing your daughter did for you. The Easterlings were Carolyn Wentworth's parents?"

The light dimmed in Anjelita's face. "Yes. It was a tragedy when they died. And now Carolyn is dead too. Another tragedy." She crossed herself.

"I understand you helped raise Carolyn."

"Yes, because her mother was an invalid. Carolyn wasn't even a year older than my Marisa, so they played together always. They were as close as sisters."

Nick wanted an opinion other than Marisa's. "Do you believe what her husband says, that she took her own life?"

"That one." Anjelita snorted. "If she died, it was probably to get away from him."

"What do you mean?" He was so surprised, the question was sharper than he intended.

"Scott Wentworth is a cold bastard, forgive me for swearing. Just ask my Marisa."

At that moment, Marisa appeared in the doorway and his mouth dried. He'd thought her a striking woman in her office clothes, but in khaki shorts and a white formfitting shirt, she was hot. She had curves in all the right places, and legs . . . God, she had legs. His manly parts that had been frustratingly unresponsive the past six months let him know they were alive and ready for action.

And then he spotted Marisa's mother. It was like being doused with ice water. He reined his hormones in fast. Marisa was not a one-night-stand and she had just been dumped. Not to mention she was grieving over her friend's recent death. Any decent, self-respecting man would understand that she was off limits to a randy mutt like him. He should be ashamed of himself.

"Are you ready?" Marisa asked.

Damn straight he was. Nick cleared his throat. "Yeah. Do you want to walk up or down the gorge?" He opened the outer door for her.

"Better make it down. I have a client later and I'd prefer not to be all sweaty."

Nick turned away from her so she wouldn't see the hunger on his face. He couldn't have picked a worse time to get his mojo back. Dammit, he'd been all but dead for months. Burnout, the department shrink had said. He'd hated being forced on leave, but maybe the time off had done some good if his libido was any indication.

They drove to the upper parking lot for the Watkins Glen gorge and he retrieved his camera from the trunk.

"How long has it been since you walked the glen?" Marisa asked.

Nick had to think about it. "Three years." The time span shocked him. "I hadn't realized it had been so long."

They began the descent into the gorge. "Did you use to visit regularly?"

The temperature cooled a bit as they entered the shade. "Every year since Brian moved here. We shared a dorm room at college and have been best friends ever since."

"Like Caro and I." Sadness filled her eyes.

"Yeah." He rushed on so Marisa wouldn't dwell on her friend. "After Brian moved here he told me how beautiful it was and I took my vacation here. I came every year after that."

"But not lately."

"No. I haven't taken a week's vacation in a long time. There's always an emergency somewhere, always someone in pain who needs my help." And here he was helping again, trying to assist Marisa with her grief.

"Your job is so stressful. You need time away to re-energize."

"That's why I'm here—mandatory time off for another week." He heard the bitterness in his voice. People were dying back home without him. Well, they were dying here, too.

Marisa walked ahead of him up steps made of the dark charcoal stone to blend in naturally with the gorge. He liked the way her shorts clung to her butt as she climbed. And then the stairway turned and he glimpsed Marisa framed against the backdrop of the gorge and all its natural beauty.

He froze, breathless from the beauty of the woman and the gorge. He'd seen nothing but ugliness for months. All the color, save red, had leeched from his world, leaving only blood, death and pain. But this scene stirred something inside him and he thought he felt the ice around his frozen soul crack.

CHAPTER 6

Marisa saw the lines of strain on Nick's face soften and knew he'd been affected by the glory of the gorge. Oddly, she felt glad his burdens were eased. His story haunted her and she was sure it haunted him. No wonder he didn't smile.

"Why don't you take a picture?" she said.

Nick shook himself like a man coming out of a trance. "Yeah. This is perfect. Stand right there." He raised the camera to his face.

"Oh no. You don't want me in the photo."

"Yes I do." He sounded fierce.

Marisa didn't argue further. She studied him as he adjusted the lens and the settings. He fumbled a little at first, but then his movements became fluid and he handled the camera with ease. She heard the shutter click twice.

"Light's not the best," he said. "Morning light is better."

That bit of knowledge wasn't something most casual photographers knew. How could he have given up a hobby he loved for work? Mandatory time off meant he was suffering from job burnout. She didn't think EMTs did their job for the money, but because they cared. What must this caring man have seen and witnessed working without a vacation for three years? Her heart bled for him.

"Have you photographed other sites in this area?" she asked.

"Some. I haven't had time before to find all the waterfalls around here. I've driven over to Montour Falls and taken pictures of the falls in town. And I've taken lots of photos of the lake."

"I could show you around." The words were out of her mouth before she could censor them. She didn't know this man. But she wanted to help bring some joy into his life. And she needed to see those beautiful places for herself. Taking Nick to them would give her an excuse.

They stood in a wide section where flat ledges and towering walls bordered the river and looked down the gorge that had been carved by the water eons ago. The afternoon sun bathed the top of the eastern side and made the water sparkle.

Marisa let the beauty of the glen massage her battered soul. She soaked in the solace of a place she felt God had built. Others might be awed by the colors of the Grand Canyon, but for staggering grandeur, it had nothing on the Watkins Glen gorge.

Like many townspeople, Kevin had taken the gorge and the waterfalls for granted. He hadn't walked the glen when he came home to visit; there had never seemed enough time. So she'd gone alone. It was the tourists like Nick who truly appreciated the sight.

Her thoughts drew her gaze to him. His face had relaxed a little. The scenery was working its magic on him too. Here was something she had in common with him. She pushed aside the problems of Carolyn and Scott and her mother. She needed time to draw breath and strength to face what was to come.

"Are you ready to go on?" Nick asked, his voice quiet.

He couldn't know what she'd been thinking, but she nodded. There was a mile left to walk, plenty of time to recharge her spirit.

Marisa didn't say a word when Nick stopped to photograph a swirl of water or a particularly pleasing stone staircase, or any of the rapids or falls in the gorge. He needed this as much as she did. She wondered if he would have come without her. For some reason, she thought not. She didn't know how long he'd been in town, but he hadn't visited the park during that time.

By the time they reached the final stone bridge and the lower parking lot, the afternoon was well advanced. Marisa had found the peace she sought. Nick seemed relaxed as well.

As they waited for the shuttle bus to transport them to the upper lot, Marisa watched the activity on Franklin Street. She'd invested in this town and she loved it here. She loved that the gorge opened onto the main road and that the town ran down to the edge of one of the Finger Lakes. She loved that wine country was right up the highway and that Watkins Glen hosted a world-class NASCAR and Indy racetrack. Tourists brought in revenue—including to her mother's shop—yet Watkins Glen remained a small town at heart. She never wanted to leave here. And she'd do everything in her power to prevent Scott Wentworth from destroying this town.

She needed to alert the other citizens to what Scott was planning. She turned to Nick. "My office is close enough to walk from here. I want to thank you for bringing me. I really needed it."

"I'm glad you could get away. It's nice to find someone who knows what to do around a photographer. Was your fiancé one?"

Some of her peace bled away. She'd forgotten her problems for several hours. "No. Watkins Glen sees a lot of tourists. I've learned how to act around people wielding cameras."

"I hurt you by bringing up your fiancé. I'm sorry."

His comment confirmed what she'd suspected about him. "It's all right. Living in a small town, I can't avoid people asking me about him."

"But I wanted to take you away from what hurts you."

The shuttle bus stopped in front of them. The few other passengers filed to the door.

"You did, Nick. Give me your phone number." He scribbled on the back of a card. "I'll call you and let you know when I can get away for a couple of hours tomorrow."

"I appreciate what you're doing for me, especially now."

"I need this as much as you do, Nick."

Marisa didn't watch the shuttle take Nick away. Instead, she crossed the street and entered the first tourist shop. She didn't know the young woman behind the counter.

"Excuse me, is Henry here?"

The clerk fetched the owner. When Henry DeSoto saw Marisa, his aging face softened with sympathy. He pulled her toward the back of the shop.

His balding head made him look like a monk, but he never wanted for an escort of either sex, even though he was openly gay.

"Marisa, darling, I was so sorry to hear about you and Kevin. You were the perfect couple. And Carolyn Wentworth." He shook his head, tsking. "I couldn't believe it, still can't believe it. You two were inseparable. You must be devastated."

Tears misted Marisa's eyes. She squeezed Henry's arm in thanks. "It's very hard right now. And, Henry, it's going to get worse." She told him about Scott's plan to sell the salt plant.

"I didn't like him. I rarely saw Carolyn smile when he was with her. It was one of those money-marries-money mergers. Poor Carolyn deserved better than that, but with her parents' marriage as her example, what could you expect? She knew she had to do her duty."

Marisa had seen firsthand the polite, civil marriage the Easterlings had, but she wouldn't discuss Carolyn's marriage. Her friend had been trashed enough already. "I'm going to have a memorial service for Carolyn this week. I'll send out details as soon as I can. Will you spread the word about the salt plant and the wake?"

"Sure, hon. What are we going to do to stop the sale? He's the majority shareholder."

"I don't know, but who knows who'd buy the plant and what changes they'd implement? A foreign conglomerate might even want it."

"We can't have that! I'll tell everyone I see. Someone will think of something."

"Thanks, Henry."

They air kissed and Marisa moved on to the next shop. She spread the word down Franklin Street and knew in this small town most of the residents would know by nightfall. Everyone she spoke to was supportive. She couldn't have loved the shop owners more and it solidified her resolve never to leave Watkins Glen.

By the time she walked in the door of her office, she felt drained but elated.

Her mother turned, her face lit with excitement. "*Mi hija*, so many people have called. They want to know if you are calling a town meeting to stop Scott from selling the plant."

There was an idea she hadn't thought of. "I don't know what I'm going to do, Mamá. I just started talking to shop owners on the way here."

"I think it is a very good idea and so like you to consider the town. See how different you are than that young woman you were in high school?"

Marisa couldn't deal with that right now. She felt raw from all the condolences she'd received. It hit her hard that after eight years as part of a couple, she was alone. She hadn't been enough for Kevin, hadn't been the right person.

"I'll call the mayor before Mr. Pipoly arrives for his appointment," Marisa said.

"Good. Maybe I should make empanadas tonight to celebrate, eh?" Anjelita kissed Marisa's cheek.

Marisa smiled. "I don't want you to go to any trouble, Mamá. I thought we'd go out to eat."

"The way the phone has rung, we will not get to eat if we go out. We will spend the time planning with other people while our good food grows cold."

"You're right. I'll help you cook."

Anjelita hummed as she stitched. Marisa looked up the mayor's number and called. The excited secretary put her through at once.

"Marisa Avalos," Amanda Bolliton said, her voice warm. "I expected your call."

"So I understand. Can we do anything legally to fight the sale of the plant? Should I ask for a town meeting?"

"Definitely. How about tomorrow night at eight?"

"That soon?"

"My phone has rung nonstop for the past hour. Some people were panicked. I heard from Mae Ellen Ferguson that the Chinese were buying the plant. The sooner we have an open forum the better. Will you be ready to present by then?"

"Me?"

"Of course. Henry DeSoto told me you started the awareness campaign."

"But I've never spoken to a crowd before."

"You're a business owner in this town. You've got a big stake in the town's success or failure. There can't be any issue more important than this one."

Marisa sighed. "You're right. I'll be ready by eight tomorrow. Thanks, Your Honor."

When Marisa hung up, her mother beamed at her. "See, you are an important part of this town. The mayor herself has asked you to speak. I am so proud of you, *mi hija*."

Marisa's smile felt strained. "Thanks, Mamá."

*

Later, as they made empanadas together in her mother's kitchen, Anjelita spoke. "You think this Nick is attractive."

Marisa blushed and hoped the heat of the kitchen hid it. "He's a good-looking man."

"He likes what he sees too. But there is darkness in him."

"I know." Marisa told her mother about Nick's job burnout.

"So he is hungry for what is good, or for what will divert his mind from what is bad."

"Mamá, you don't have to worry about me. I don't intend to have an affair with him." But her lower body clenched against her will.

Her mother seemed to look inward. "Sometimes attraction is so intense you cannot help yourself."

"Is that how it was with my father?"

Anjelita looked at her with sad eyes. "You are old enough now, *mi hija*, I think you will understand. I was new to this town and alone for the first time in my life. All the men thought I was beautiful. They paid attention to me. It went to my head. But they only wanted my body. It made me felt even more alone. I am ashamed at how I came to know carnal love and with how many men. I wanted to be loved, you see.

"When I was at my loneliest, I met a man who set my body aflame with his touch. I gave myself to him, and I gave him my heart. I would have done anything for him, *mi hija*, even though I knew it was wrong. I let him use me because I loved him."

Marisa's throat felt tight. "And then he left you."

Her mother's answer came slowly. "Yes. I love him still. I shall never love another man like that."

"But he deserted you."

Her mother clasped Marisa's hands in hers. "Oh, *mi hija*, how can I make you understand?"

"You can't." Marisa pulled her hands away and swallowed through a tight throat. "Did he know about me?"

Her mother looked down, tucking the last empanada carefully into the oven dish. "He knew."

"So he deserted me too. And yet you still love him." All this time Marisa had suspected her father's desertion was because of her mother's pregnancy—because of *her*. Now was the perfect time to ask, but she couldn't bring herself to confirm it.

"Do not let this Nick do that to you, *mi hija*. There is such intensity about him. I think he could be one whose touch is like flame. And he is not here to stay. I do not wish to see your heart broken again."

"Mamá, do you wish you'd never met my father?"

Anjelita shook her head. "No, *mi hija*. To feel a love like that is not to be missed. Besides, I was blessed with you."

Marisa squeezed her mother's hand. "But he didn't really love you, Mamá. He couldn't have."

"He did, as much as he was able. That is why I love him still."

Her mother and father's strange relationship consumed Marisa's thoughts later as she left her mother's cottage and took the shortcut across the big house grounds. A breeze blew from the west, making the tree branches sway and chasing the few fallen leaves across her path. The quarter moon showed through the leaves and cast ghostly moving shadows.

A chill roughened the skin on Marisa's forearms. The brisk fall evening was a sharp contrast to the hot day and the heat in her mother's kitchen. But it was a beautiful night to walk the half mile to her apartment. The sky was clear, without the glare and pollution of big city lights and smog. She sucked in the crisp, fresh air. Down the hill, a truck changed gears as it climbed out of the valley.

A shadow darkened the path and leaves crackled. Marisa's neck prickled. She whirled to face whomever it might be, her key gripped like a weapon in her hand. But the lawn behind her was empty, the trees silent sentinels to the night.

Marisa's heart pounded. She could swear she hadn't been alone. A cloud moved across the crescent of the moon as she scanned the trees, but when the area was once again bathed in gentle moonlight, she still saw no one.

Turning, she hurried toward the road. She was just rattled from the events of the day. Ghosts haunted her tonight.

As the road heaved into sight through the front gate, a breeze chased leaves around her feet. Tree branches swayed alarmingly. The hairs on her neck stood out. Marisa sprinted the last hundred yards. She couldn't hear anything over her pounding feet and heart. Was someone running too? She dare not turn around to see.

She flashed through the brick posts that bracketed the Easterling driveway and reached the streetlight. Swiveling, she planted her feet to attack. But there was no one there. Her gaze jerked right and left as she gulped breath into her heaving lungs. Her heart continued to thud too loudly to hear anything else. The trees still swayed in the breeze. Leaves danced. But no human moved among the shadows.

Marisa swung in the other direction and scrutinized her surroundings. No one jumped out at her. Still, she couldn't shake her uneasiness, even though it was just the wind. She hurried down the center of the street toward her apartment. She hated being afraid for apparently no reason.

CHAPTER 7

By mid-morning the next day, Marisa felt she'd spoken to half the townspeople about the upcoming meeting. She understood why they couldn't wait until that night to find out the details, but she wasn't getting any work done. And she hadn't had a chance to speak to her mother about her strange uneasiness last night.

When the phone rang again, she dreaded answering but did.

"It's Nick Stark. Do you have a place picked out to photograph?"

Chagrined, she grimaced. "Oh, Nick, I'm so sorry. I forgot all about it with the town meeting coming up."

"That's okay. Maybe some other time." His response sounded too bright and forced.

At that moment, she decided her work could wait. She wanted to watch him take photographs again. Maybe he might loosen up enough to smile. "No, no. I'll come get you right now. I need a break from all these phone calls."

"I can drive." He sounded eager.

But Marisa had a better idea. "Let me drive so you can take pictures along the way."

"Okay. I'm renting a cabin on Salt Point Road." He gave her the address.

"I'll be there in about ten minutes. We'll drive up through the wineries on the west side of the lake. It's beautiful country."

"It sounds great."

No sooner had Marisa hung up then the phone rang again. Thinking Nick had forgotten something, she answered with, "Don't worry about lunch. We'll stop along the way."

"Miss Avalos?" The woman's voice was familiar, but Marisa couldn't place it.

"Yes?"

"It's Grace Vanaker, the general manager's secretary at the plant. I'm calling to notify you of a stockholder's meeting at three." Grace sounded harried.

"So soon?" Scott sure didn't waste any time.

"Mr. Wentworth called an emergency meeting."

Her chest muscles constricted. Scott was going to beat them to the punch. Her mind scrambled for a reason to delay until after tonight's town meeting, but she could think of nothing. She sighed. "Where's it to be held?"

"In the conference room at the plant."

"I'll be there." She hung up, but her anger and frustration boiled over. Her fists clenched on the desktop. "Damn Scott Wentworth!"

"What has he done now, *mi hija*?"

"Called an emergency board meeting. He must have heard about the town meeting tonight and he's trying to outmaneuver us."

"Surely he will not be able to sell the plant today?"

"Not sell it, no. But he'll try to pass a motion to put the plant on the market. I've got to stop him, but I only own a few shares. Damn, I'll have to call Nick back and cancel." Disappointment weighted her down and took some of the brightness from the day. How strange that the planned time with Nick seemed so important to her.

"You are tired, *mi hija*. There are dark circles under your eyes. Surely you will fight better if you take a few hours to plan what you will say."

Marisa wondered why her mother was pushing her into Nick's company when she'd already warned Marisa about him. But she was too stressed to come up with an answer. Besides, the glow had returned to the day. So she turned on the answering machine, kissed her mother good-bye and headed down the road to Nick's cabin. Her heart beat faster and her breathing accelerated the closer she got to his road. She tried but failed to tamp down an almost giddy eagerness.

Nick was just as darkly appealing as he'd been the other times she'd seen him. He wore a white T-shirt that stretched across his wide chest and faded blue jeans that hugged his narrow hips. He looked great. Marisa's mouth dried. Again, she felt guilty about the strength of her attraction to him.

Nick climbed in her car and suddenly the front seat wasn't big enough. She was acutely aware of his body heat and the fresh outdoorsy scent that clung to him. Her clothes felt too tight and her palms were moist on the steering wheel.

"I'm glad you could spare the time." His deep voice vibrated the air between them and her lower body clenched in response.

Marisa managed a coherent reply, even though her brain was processing on the most primal of levels. "You gave me an excuse to get away from all the phone calls." As they headed up Route 14, she filled him in on the town meeting and the upcoming stockholder's meeting.

He frowned. "One man wields a lot of power over your town."

"It was different when Andrew Easterling owned everything. He was one of us."

Nick turned in his seat to face her. "You knew him well?"

"I spent half my life at the big house with Carolyn. She spent the other half at mine. So when Mr. Easterling played with her, he played with me too. Carolyn's mom was an invalid, so he taught us to ride bikes, how to skate, and how to drive a car. In a way, he was the dad I never had, and my mom was the mother figure Carolyn's mom couldn't be."

"Was he at your house a lot?"

"He was our landlord and Mama's employer, and his daughter spent half her days at our house. Of course, he was there. I saw him every day except when he was out of town. Why are you asking?" She narrowed her eyes at him, an ugly suspicion forming.

He confirmed it. "I've heard rumors your mother was more than his employee."

"It's a lie. My mother is still in love with my father. She's never even looked at another man." She felt oddly hurt by his doubt.

"Sorry. I just wondered if Andrew Easterling might have been your father."

Marisa's hands gripped the steering wheel until they hurt. "No. My father left town before Mamá went to work for the Easterlings."

A tense silence filled the car. Her mother's words from yesterday sprang into Marisa's mind. She'd known a lot of carnal love before Marisa's father. Would her mother have needed sex after she'd been deserted? And there was Andrew Easterling with a newly paralyzed wife looking to assuage a need.

Marisa shuddered. Before yesterday, she never would have entertained the idea. But yesterday her body had come alive near Nick, and today it was even worse. Apparently a woman could be in love with one man and still desire another. But she was stronger than her desire. She burned with shame.

"I'm sorry," he said again. "I spoiled our day."

Marisa glanced at him and saw the concern in his dark eyes. She swallowed her retort. "It's a hard time for everyone right now and Scott is making it worse. Here's the first winery."

Nick looked like he wanted to say more, but Marisa parked the car and strode to stand looking down the hill. Nick stood beside her, his camera clasped in his hands.

The straight rows of vines soothed her logical mind. The blue backdrop of Seneca Lake calmed her agitated emotions. The pastoral scene eased the knots of tension from her tight muscles. The quiet clicking of the camera's shutter did nothing to disturb the scene.

Nick lowered his camera. "I knew there were wineries around here, but I never thought of seeing one."

"There are twenty-eight around Seneca Lake, each one a different style. I wish we had time to drive up to Belhurst on the tip of the lake so you could photograph the castle."

His brown eyes gleamed with eagerness. "How long would it take?"

"If we don't stop at any other wineries, about forty minutes."

Nick's mouth kicked up on one side, displaying a dimple.

Marisa's breath stalled in her throat. What would it be like to see a full smile? Half of her wanted to, while the other half was afraid what would happen if she did.

*

The drive up the lake was beautiful and soothing. When he saw the castle, Nick sucked in his breath. "Is that it?"

His excitement sparked Marisa's. "Yes, beautiful, isn't it."

"Oh yes." He gripped his camera.

As she watched Nick photograph the castle and vineyards, Marisa knew she'd chosen correctly. Slowly, the lines of strain drained from his face and his dimple flashed more often. She had to look away because she was finding him too damned attractive.

She and Kevin had come here long ago, two high school seniors in the rush of dating euphoria. He'd played the knight, gallantly showing her Belhurst. They hadn't been able to afford a room at the castle, so she'd rewarded him her virginity that night in his car by the lake. In retrospect, their passionate fumbling seemed almost comical. Kevin had gone off to college soon afterwards. Had they ever gotten to know one another deeper than that?

"Marisa?"

She'd been staring at the castle, remembering. She jerked herself free of the past and turned to Nick. The lines of strain in his face had doubled.

"I have something to tell you. I was waiting for the right time, but now it seems a poor reward for bringing me here."

Marisa's chest tightened. What else could go wrong? She braced herself for whatever it was.

"I know a lot of medical people in New York City. This morning I called a friend who called a friend—Carolyn's psychiatrist."

Marisa sucked in her breath. Her body tensed with dread.

"The psychiatrist could talk to my friend only because Carolyn is dead. She did come to him for depression after a miscarriage . . . "

"Oh God!" Marisa's hand flew to her mouth. Tears welled in her eyes. His words were like stakes pounded into her heart.

" . . . But it was five months ago. He'd released her from his care."

Five months ago. What was the significance of that timeframe? Five months ago, it had been May. May, and Kevin had graduated and come home. Marisa had thought her life could begin at last. She could settle down with a husband to become two distinguished pillars of the community. They could finally begin their own dynasty. She remembered babbling her happy news to Carolyn on the phone.

Tears overflowed and ran down her cheeks. The scenery in front of her blurred into a kaleidoscope of colors. "It's my fault." Scott Wentworth had been right, damn him!

"What's your fault?" Nick's words were sharp.

"That she had no one to talk to. She couldn't talk to me—her best friend—because Kevin had just come home after eight years at college. I talked nonstop about getting married and how happy I was." Marisa turned to Nick and sobbed. "She didn't want to rain on my parade. She was hurting and she couldn't even tell me. Scott told me yesterday, but I didn't believe him."

Nick captured one of her tight fists. "Your friend sought a professional, which was the right thing to do. Didn't you hear me? He helped her. He'd released her."

But Marisa shook her head and pulled her hand away from his much warmer one, turning to face the lake. "What did being here and seeing me do to her? Did it remind her of what she'd lost?" Guilt made her stomach cramp and burn.

Nick stroked her back with a gentle circling motion. "I thought you said she wasn't the type to kill herself?"

She should refuse his touch. She didn't deserve his gentleness. "Nothing is what it seemed. Once there wasn't a secret Carolyn and I didn't share."

"You grew up and became adults." His voice soothed.

"And then she moved away and left me behind." Bitterness welled up, at herself, at Carolyn. "She got married, became a member of New York society."

"You envied her." Nick kept his voice gentle. "That's very human."

"She was my best friend! How sick was it to be jealous of her happiness? I had a boyfriend." The anger inside her spilled out.

"Who was away at college. A husband is different than a boyfriend."

"We got engaged after Carolyn got married." Oh God, the timing slapped her in the face. It was a pity engagement. Kevin had tried to make her feel better because her best friend had gotten married. Marisa felt sick. She hadn't been able to let go of the people she loved. Scott had said Carolyn hadn't made new friends in New York City because Marisa had held on. And Kevin had learned to love city life, but Marisa wouldn't let him go. Now Caro was dead and Kevin was moving away.

Nick took hold of her forearms so she had to face him. His jaw looked hard as granite. "What happened to your friend wasn't your fault. It more than likely wasn't her fault. Didn't you hear what I said? Scott Wentworth lied about when his wife saw a shrink. The psychiatrist hadn't prescribed Carolyn antidepressants in months, but Wentworth said she was taking them. Why did he lie?"

Marisa sniffed back her sobs. "Could there be another psychiatrist?"

"I asked my friend to ask around. No one had a patient named Carolyn Wentworth."

"What are you saying? If she didn't jump in front of the train . . . " Marisa sucked in her breath, unable to continue.

"Either she stumbled, or Scott Wentworth pushed her."

CHAPTER 8

"Scott Wentworth pushed Carolyn in front of the train?" Marisa repeated. It was too horrible, too inconceivable that even Scott could do that. "Why?"

"Money, for one," Nick said. "He inherited a business and valuable real estate, didn't he?"

"I can't believe it." Yet hadn't Scott begrudged her the few items Carolyn had willed her?

"You've been adamant that Carolyn didn't kill herself. That only leaves two choices. You've got to admit the possibility that Scott might have wanted his wife out of the way."

"Did you tell Deputy Nash what the psychiatrist said?"

"I felt you should know first. Besides, the sheriff doesn't want Scott Wentworth 'bothered.' The sheriff told Brian to close the case with a verdict of suicide."

Marisa sucked in her breath. "Which would allow a killer to go free, if Scott killed her." No. She couldn't allow that to happen.

Nick nodded. "If he did it. She could have fallen trying to reach whatever she'd dropped, like the one eyewitness said."

"If she did drop something, it's long gone. The town prides itself on a clean promenade."

"There's no harm in looking."

"Then we should start back now." Marisa turned toward the car.

Nick halted her with a hand on her arm. "I can't tell you how sorry I am that I ruined our day. This was a beautiful place and I appreciate you sharing it with me."

Marisa stared into the depths of his chocolate brown eyes and felt herself drowning. Her lips parted, drawing his gaze. She moistened them and watched desire heat his eyes. Her body thrummed with a corresponding need. She wanted him to peel off her clothes and lick everything he found underneath until she lay boneless and sated beneath him.

God, what was she thinking! She tore her gaze from his. Only last week she'd shared her fiancé's bed for one of their lukewarm sexual encounters. Even the actual act with Kevin didn't compare to the heat of a daydream about Nick. What was wrong with her?

She hurried to the car and knew Nick followed. But as she opened the door and turned, she was abruptly plastered against his body. He grabbed her arms to prevent her from stumbling. An electric shock went through her body and centered in her lower belly. She felt desperate to be intimately filled with him. Her panties dampened and her nipples peaked.

"You don't have to be afraid of me," Nick breathed into her ear. His erection pressed against her stomach.

Oh yes she did. She wanted him to mount her right here on the lawn of Belhurst and ride her hard and fast. She wanted to cry "Harder!"—something she'd never done with Kevin, the man she supposedly loved.

"Please." Her voice sounded breathy. She wasn't even sure now what she was begging him for. She pressed her thighs against his.

"You're safe with me. I won't hurt you." He cupped her face and raised it to his.

Marisa saw brown eyes instead of blue, dark hair instead of fair, intensity instead of placidness. Distance. She needed distance. "You live in New York City."

The passion cooled in his eyes, slowly replaced by the deadness she'd seen in them that first day. She hadn't meant to do that.

Nick peeled his body from hers. Hers clung; so did his. She felt chilled when he no longer blanketed her.

"I'm sorry." His voice sounded flat and emotionless. "It wasn't my intention to bring you here to seduce you. My father taught me how to treat women with respect."

Although she'd wanted distance, she hadn't wanted to hurt him. "It's all right. Let's go back to town so we can look for whatever Carolyn dropped."

"Sure." Nick looked like he wanted to say more, but he closed his mouth and climbed into the car.

As Marisa navigated Route 14 back to Watkins Glen, she pondered what she'd learned while pressed against Nick's firm body. She was attracted to the flame, and Nick was an inferno. If she wasn't careful, she was going to get burned.

*

Nick glanced again and again at Marisa's strained profile. He'd done that, stressed her by pressing the mutual attraction they shared. Even now it was uncomfortable to sit in the car with a killer hard-on. He wanted her like he'd never wanted another woman. He could have ravished her right there at Belhurst in broad daylight.

She was everything a man could want in a partner: intelligent, caring, community-minded, a loyal friend, a loving daughter, beautiful, sexy, and full of life. He hungered to possess her vitality. She made him feel alive again, and he didn't want to go back to the dark deadness that had been his life for so many months.

Yet she was right. His life wasn't here and hers was. He couldn't ruin what she had in Watkins Glen by sating both their sexual needs. She was hurting and in need of comfort. She didn't need a fiery sexual liaison.

Yes she did. And so did he. But he couldn't do that to her. That would hurt her.

She drove into the parking lot of the restaurant where they'd witnessed her friend's death. Together they crisscrossed the area surrounding the promenade for twenty minutes before accepting that Marisa was right—there was no trash of any kind on or near the railroad crossing. If Carolyn had dropped something, the town of Watkins Glen was too thorough in cleaning the scene.

"Do you really think Carolyn dropping something?" Marisa asked.

Nick ran a frustrated hand through his hair. "I don't know. Eyewitness accounts are known to contradict one another."

"Then it's a dead end." She winced when she said it and looked out over the lake. Then she frowned. "I wonder what's going on out there."

There seemed to be a lot of activity in the harbor. A number of boats were heading out. Nick knew a situation response when he saw one. He spotted Brian directing.

"C'mon. We'll find out."

They reached his buddy just as another boat sped away from the dock.

"What's happening?" Nick asked.

Brian looked up from his clipboard. "The salt plant's intake pipe is blocked. Production's been halted. I'm sending out every licensed diver. Do you dive, Nick?" He looked hopeful.

Nick shook his head. "Nope."

"Too bad. I need every able-bodied hand."

"Deputy, don't you think the timing's a bit coincidental?" Marisa asked. "There are two meetings concerning the plant today."

Brian glanced from her to Nick. Nick wasn't sure if he saw a question in his friend's eyes before the deputy answered Marisa.

"You think someone purposely stopped production?"

"I don't know. Have you checked Scott Wentworth's whereabouts?"

"Miss Avalos, Scott Wentworth owns the plant. He wants to sell it. He's not going to sabotage it. And it's probably not a good idea for you to make unfounded accusations against him."

Marisa raised her stubborn chin. "I'm not afraid of Scott Wentworth. Do I have a reason to be?"

Again Brian glanced at Nick. Nick shrugged. "Tell her why she should fear her best friend's husband."

"That's not what I meant and you know it."

"Nick, tell him about the psychiatrist," Marisa said.

Nick told his friend what he'd learned and the conclusions he and Marisa had drawn. When he finished, Brian wore a fierce frown.

"Why didn't you bring this to me first?"

"Because you're afraid of Scott and I'm not. It's a motive," Nick said.

"It deserves to be investigated," Marisa said. "I'll do it if you don't."

"All right." Brian sounded harried. He lowered his voice. "But I won't tell the sheriff. He knows who holds the money power in this town. I'll make some calls. But you'd better keep quiet about your suspicions. You don't want Wentworth to run."

Marisa straightened and lifted her chin. "I'm going up against him twice today. If I have to use what I know about him to fight him, I will."

"But you have no proof he actually pushed his wife," Brian said. "Just that he lied. She could have tripped. You can't make false accusations against him."

"Fine. I'll heed your warning. For now." Marisa turned to Nick. "I enjoyed our time together. We'll go out again tomorrow."

For a charged moment everything buzzed between them—the possibilities and the problems. His desire for her was a living, breathing thing. His offer of himself, his body, was there, unspoken.

All that existed was Marisa and her fire. He wanted to warm himself in it. He wanted the flames to consume him.

Marisa took a step back, breaking the tableau. Then she walked back to her car.

"Whew!" Brian exclaimed. "What's going on between the two of you?"

"Nothing." Everything. Nick had found life again, but when he left at the end of this week, he'd leave it behind.

"She's vulnerable."

Nick rubbed his forehead. "I know."

"So are you."

Nick's gaze jerked to his friend's. "What are you talking about?"

"Nick, this is the most like yourself you've been since you got here. I barely knew you when you arrived. There was no joy in you at all, no life. Now I can almost see the man I went to college with. And it's due to her. Marisa Avalos is passionate and alive. You're vulnerable to that right now."

"I won't give up spending time with her, if that's what you're asking." It was a solemn oath.

"I'm just saying be careful, for both your sakes."

*

When Marisa walked through her office door, her mother nearly bounced with excitement. "Grace at the plant called to say the stockholder's meeting is postponed until tomorrow due to trouble at the plant. I heard the intake pipe is blocked."

"Thank God. I've just come from the docks where Deputy Nash is sending out divers."

Anjelita hugged herself. "Our prayers are answered. The town meeting will be held first and we will find a way to stop Scott."

"I hope so." Marisa debated telling her mother what she'd learned today, but decided her mother should enjoy her moment of happiness.

CHAPTER 9

Nick climbed the front steps of the huge Victorian that housed Marisa's apartment. The street of old houses this high up on the hillside commanded an excellent view of the harbor. He wondered if this big house reminded her of the Easterling estate where she'd grown up.

He should have called to tell her he was coming over. But he felt nervous, like she'd say no. He just wanted to accompany her to the town meeting. What was wrong with that?

The front screen door was ajar a few inches. His city-bred security consciousness was appalled. But this was Watkins Glen where they had very little crime. He decided to go up to Marisa's apartment instead of buzzing her from outside.

As he put his foot on the first riser, he heard a door close above him and light quick footsteps coming down the stairs. Marisa. His heart rate sped up. He couldn't believe how eager he was to see her.

She rounded the landing into view, looking alive with vitality. She wore a blue-flowered dress that made her look very feminine. Her eyes widened when she saw him and she smiled. His breath caught and his heart took wing.

As she stepped down, he noticed something small and round on the stairs. All her concentration was on him. Before he could shout an alarm, Marisa's foot hit it and she pitched forward.

With a surge of adrenalin, Nick sprang toward Marisa, desperate to catch her before she hit her head as she fell. He leaped the last three steps and grasped her out-flung arms, using her downward momentum to pull her body against his. She hit him with an oomph that propelled him backwards. His back hit the floor with a painful thud, and her body slammed against his front with an almost equal force.

He lay there winded, staring up at the high wood ceiling and trying to calm his speeding pulse. She was safe! He looked at her and managed words. "You could have broken your neck. Thank God I was here."

She lifted her head and blew a lock of black hair out of her face. "Thanks for catching me."

"You scared me."

"You? My heart's beating like a runaway train."

He became aware that she was lying between his spread legs with her dress up around her thighs, her breasts pressed against his ribs, his cock against her stomach. He felt himself harden.

Marisa's eyes widened and she scrambled off him, wincing as she moved.

Nick climbed to his feet, hiding his own wince. He reached for her as he rose. "Are you hurt? Is anything broken? Remember I'm a paramedic."

She let him palpate her left forearm and bicep. "I don't think anything's broken. I must have hit the wall or banister when I fell."

He sighed with relief and tried not to be affected by touching her soft skin. "No, nothing's broken, but you're going to have a couple of nasty bruises. You're lucky. It could have been much worse."

"I know. Thanks again." Her voice was slightly breathy and the dark pools of her eyes held the same awareness of him that he felt. "How about you? Are you hurt? You took the brunt of our fall." Her hands fluttered as though she wasn't sure about touching him as he'd touched her.

Nick tried to control the wildfire raging inside of him. He wanted her to touch him, wanted to take Marisa in his arms and press her body all along the line of his once more. She'd been in danger and he wanted to use his hands to feel every inch of her body to confirm that she was all right. He imagined her doing the same to him and stifled a groan of need. He tried to remember that he was leaving in a week and Marisa was staying, and that she'd been engaged until recently.

He cleared his throat and stepped away from her. "You shouldn't leave things on the stairs."

"I didn't. I came home less than two hours ago and those stairs were clear. What was it anyway?" She glanced around for the object.

Nick searched until he spotted it down the hall. He scooped up the red and blue ball and handed it to her. "It was hard to see against the dark wood."

Marisa frowned. "No children live here. The nearest family lives two doors down."

"The screen door was open when I got here. I bet this is a great place to play."

"Not if the children are going to leave their toys for someone to trip on. I'll have to speak to them tomorrow." Her gaze tangled with his once more and she smiled. "What are you doing here?"

Nerves fluttered in his stomach. "Besides rescuing you, I was hoping you'd let me escort you to the town meeting. I've never been to one."

"Some of it might not be pleasant. The townspeople are upset."

"I live in New York City. People there can get pretty unpleasant."

Marisa brushed herself off and tidied her hair. "Don't say I didn't warn you."

He followed her out the door, making sure the screen latched behind him. When she let him seat her in his car, he felt he'd won. She directed him down the steep hill toward Franklin Street to the town hall offices. He parked the car and came around to open her door.

"Did you bring your camera?" she asked.

"Nope. I'm just observing tonight." His hand itched to touch the small of her back, but he resisted.

Marisa licked her lips. His eyes followed the movement that his tongue wanted to trace. She saw where he was staring, and when she spoke next, her voice was nervous and fast.

"I'm going to be at the podium. You're welcome to sit with me if you like."

"In the spotlight?" He tried to lighten things. "No thanks."

It worked. Marisa responded easily to his banter. "Chicken."

"That's me." He saw a determined looking woman advancing with purpose toward them. Their time alone was about to come to an end. "I'll drive you home afterwards."

She shook her head. "You don't have to."

"I want to." He needed to.

"All right."

"Marisa," the woman greeted her with enthusiasm. "Are you ready?" She was fifty-ish, blonde, and self-confident. Her sand-colored pantsuit and white pearls looked elegant on her.

"Yes, Your Honor, I am." Marisa introduced them. "Mrs. Mayor, this is Nick Stark. Nick, Mayor Amanda Bolliton."

"Your Honor." Nick shook her proffered hand.

He could practically see her thinking. "You're Deputy Nash's friend."

He raised an eyebrow in surprise. "You're well informed."

"I try to be. Marisa, the problem at the plant today makes this meeting critical. I have the report on the cause of the blockage and it wasn't natural."

"Sabotage?" Nick said.

"Yes." Mrs. Bolliton nodded. "This is serious. I've told Sheriff Kehr to make it his top priority to find the culprit or culprits."

That would work right into the sheriff's plan to close the Wentworth case. Nick caught Marisa's eye to see if she realized it.

She did. "What about Carolyn Wentworth's case?"

The mayor frowned at Marisa. "Sheriff Kehr said it was a suicide."

"It wasn't." Marisa words carried flat resolve.

"Oh dear. I'll speak to the sheriff, but he has so little manpower."

Nick thought of a solution. "Mrs. Mayor, if you'd tell the sheriff that it's all right for Brian Nash to keep investigating Mrs. Wentworth's death in his free time, I think that would satisfy Miss Avalos."

Marisa gave him a quick look of gratitude, "Yes, Your Honor, I'd be grateful. I loved Carolyn like a sister. I don't want her death to go unsolved."

The mayor nodded her blonde head. "Consider it taken care of."

When the mayor entered the building ahead of them, Marisa's smile made Nick's stomach do a funny flip. It was the first real smile he'd seen. It lit up her face and he saw how truly alive she was.

He felt like a star struck fan as he followed her into the town hall. Even as early as they were, the hall was filled with people sitting, standing, and talking.

Heads turned toward the mayor and then to Marisa. People moved to speak to her as she passed, Nick following in her wake like a boat in tow. She was amazing and so unlike the woman he'd seen that first day. She was full of vital energy and purpose. He'd seen glimpses of it in her defense of her friend. She greeted many people by name, shook hands with everyone who stopped her, and listened to what people had to say.

Marisa introduced him to a lot of people. He wondered what it would be like to be her other half. Nick saw only desirable qualities. What had her fiancé seen or not seen in her to make him throw her away? Nick felt like punching the other man for his stupidity and for hurting Marisa. Oddly enough, it was the latter that made him angrier.

At eight o'clock, the mayor took her place at the podium and brought silence to the assembly. Nick didn't see an empty seat in the hall. He also didn't see Scott Wentworth or Kevin Johansson. Nick nodded to Brian as his friend slid in the door. Brian saluted him with two fingers and then leaned against the wall.

"We all know what this meeting is about," Mayor Bolliton began. "But let's hear it firsthand from the woman who will save our town, Marisa Avalos."

There was loud applause and then Marisa took over the podium.

"Most of you know me or have seen me. I was born here twenty-six years ago. My mom's been here nearly thirty." Marisa smiled to her left and Nick saw her mother wave.

"I've built my business here and so has my mom. We're part of this town and we like it here. We don't want it to change. You've all heard how Carolyn Wentworth died." She choked, and her eyes filled. She cleared her throat and proceeded.

"Now Scott Wentworth owns everything and he intends to sell it. He doesn't care to whom or how it gets sold as long as someone takes the plant off his hands quickly."

There was a murmur of discontent from the crowd.

"A lot of you work there."

"Yeah!" numerous voices responded.

"And I want you to keep your jobs . . . "

The responses were louder this time.

"Local jobs for local people."

"You got that right!" one man shouted.

"I need to hear your ideas of what we can do to keep those jobs right here in Watkins Glen. The mayor will entertain any idea, as long as it's legal."

Mayor Bolliton joined Marisa at the podium. Nick could picture Marisa becoming mayor when she was Amanda Bolliton's age. They were two women connected intimately to this town.

One by one, the townspeople stood and offered ideas, including the workers buying out Scott Wentworth. Other people offered opinions or stories about the plant or Mr. Easterling.

A short barrage of Andrew Easterling anecdotes followed, and then one wrinkled man stood and shouted in a carrying voice, "Why don't you dispute the will?"

"How?"

"How do you think?"

Marisa frowned. "You'll have to be more specific."

"You're the old man's bastard. Just ask for what's yours."

Nick stiffened. Several responses of "Yeah, it's yours" followed the first man's, but the majority of people were silent. Marisa's face reddened. Nick glanced at her mother to find she'd paled. How humiliating for her.

"I'm not Andrew Easterling's child," Marisa said.

"I helped Andrew Easterling move your ma from her tiny apartment to his estate. He was familiar with that apartment and with your ma. And it wasn't seven months later that you were born."

"He was not my father."

"It's easy enough to prove," someone else shouted. "Get a DNA test."

"Yeah," several people agreed.

"We don't have time to waste on useless things," Marisa said. "Especially when I know the outcome won't be positive."

A young, well-dressed man stood. "The test could hold up the disposition of the will, especially since so many of us are sure the results will be positive."

Marisa looked strained now. Her mother had her face in her hands. Nick felt like an ass for having asked Marisa if the rumors were true. Had she heard them all her life? Why were the townspeople so sure she was Easterling's child? Did some of them know things they were too discreet to say?

All he was sure of was that he needed to rescue Marisa. He stepped away from the wall. "What about passing a law about who can own the plant? That you have to be a New York resident or something?"

"It's possible," Mayor Bolliton said. "What about it, Mr. Jantzen?"

The well-dressed man responded, "I'll have to research it, Your Honor."

"Then do so. Can I have your answer tomorrow?"

Jantzen smiled. "I'll do my best."

"Are there any other ideas?" the mayor asked.

A woman near Nick grumbled, "All she has to do is have the test."

Other ideas were tossed out and debated.

Finally, the mayor raised her hand. "I think we have enough ideas. There's one more issue we need to discuss—what happened at the plant today." She silenced the murmurs again. "Someone intentionally blocked the intake pipe."

People gasped. "What?"

"Who?" others asked.

"Did Wentworth do it? Is he trying to sabotage the plant?" one old woman asked.

"We don't know who did it," the mayor said. "But we're going to find out. And security is going to be increased at the plant to prevent any other incidents."

"Do you expect more sabotage?" someone shouted.

"Why don't you just arrest Wentworth?" the old woman who thought he was the saboteur asked.

"If you have any information, please tell the sheriff."

The meeting degenerated into a shouting match when someone mentioned starting a vigilante patrol. Nick noted the tense stances of Brian, the sheriff, and the other deputies, and decided he'd better get Marisa out of there.

He headed for the podium, but it seemed others had the same idea. From the corner of his eye he saw Marisa's mother—still unmoving in a sea of flowing bodies—and he headed for her.

People touched her arm or shoulder as they passed, but it was as though everyone was afraid to speak to her after the accusations that had been made.

Nick placed his hand on her shoulder and gently spoke her name. "Anjelita."

Her hands dropped from her face and she looked up. A wealth of emotions crossed her still-beautiful face. Her lips were framed to speak a name, but it wasn't his, and the moment she recognized him it went unspoken.

Nick's breath seized in his throat. He tried not to let the awareness of the name reach his face. There were enough rumors in this hall already.

"Anjelita, let me take you home."

Her hand covered his on her shoulder. "Thank you, but I need to speak with my daughter. She can drive me home."

"I drove her here."

"Oh." Anjelita looked cornered, glancing around until her gaze fixed on something. Then her face softened but her eyes were sad. "My daughter should have had a name. Then her proudest moment would not be spoiled by what people say."

Nick sat beside her in the straight chair and lowered his voice. "You could have given her her father's name. It's legal in this state."

There was such pain in Anjelita's eyes that Nick reached out to grip her hand. A man would sell his soul to make this woman happy. What had Andrew Easterling sold? He'd taken a beautiful young woman who was nearly two months pregnant to his estate to become his housekeeper and he'd kept her there for more than a quarter century. Had Anjelita not been happy there, she would have left. But she hadn't. Had Andrew Easterling provided the tie that kept her there, a biological tie?

"I could not do that," Anjelita whispered so low Nick barely heard her.

"Mamá," Marisa said from over their heads. "I'll walk you home."

"I can drive you both," Nick said. "It's too late at night to walk home, even if this is Watkins Glen."

Marisa looked like she wanted to argue, but her face also looked strained. She nodded.

Nick helped Anjelita rise. He should feel conceited to escort the two most beautiful women in the room. Instead, he felt extremely protective. These women were hurting. They needed his help.

When a man approached them as they reached the doors, Nick glared him away. Marisa and her mother couldn't take any more.

But the lawyer, Jantzen, waylaid them outside the hall. "It's in Watkins Glen's best interests if you have the test done, Miss Avalos. The hospital in Montour Falls can have the results to us quickly. I'll leave a standing order with their lab that they're to rush the test as soon as you arrive. I can file a motion for a restraining order with the court tomorrow. I know you want what's best for the town."

"Why won't you believe me?"

Jantzen's eyes went to Anjelita. "Because your mother hasn't denied it. Take the test and save the town." Then he turned on his heel and walked away.

This was no place for these two women. Nick herded them to his car, put them in the back seat together and followed Marisa's directions to her mother's home. There were many lights on at the big white house.

"Scott's working late." There was a bitter edge to Marisa's voice.

"He does not belong there," her mother said.

In the glow from the streetlight, Nick saw that both women's attention was fixed on the house. The Easterling fascination again.

He turned into the drive and followed the winding road to the pretty white cottage where Marisa had grown up. Had she grown up under her father's nose?

Nick noted that Anjelita didn't use a house key to enter the cottage. He didn't like the lack of security so close to Scott Wentworth, but how should he broach the subject?

Marisa turned in the doorway to block his entrance. "Thanks so much for the ride, Nick. I really appreciate your bringing my mother home."

He knew a dismissal when he heard one. "Do you want me to come back later to get you? I don't think you should walk home."

"I've been doing it for years." But the strain in her face and voice belied her words.

"It's no trouble for me to come get you." He couldn't bear for their time together to end like this, not when she needed comfort.

"I don't know how long I'll be."

"It doesn't matter. I'm not busy."

"Nick, please. I don't think I'll be fit company later and I don't want to fall apart on you." Her face was strained.

"Okay. But be careful walking home, and tell your mother to start locking her doors."

Marisa glanced toward the direction of the big white house and her eyes widened. "Oh. I'll tell her."

Then there was nothing left to say. Still, Nick stood in the doorway. The evening didn't seem over yet. He wanted— needed—to hold Marisa and kiss her sensual lips. He wanted to do much more than that, but kissing seemed the more desperate need. He leaned toward her. He thought she might have moved an infinitesimal bit toward him. Her lips parted. He could practically taste their sweetness, feel their warm fullness under his.

"Goodnight." Marisa backed up and closed the door.

Nick could only step out into the rapidly cooling night. He felt shut out in more ways than one. He stood in the darkness feeling desire and something else burn inside him. He knew he'd be more troubled by the unnamed need than by his unfulfilled lust.

*

"Mamá, what was my father's name?" Marisa spoke the question that throbbed between her and her mother.

Anjelita seemed to have folded in on herself. She looked so small in her favorite green rocker. "What good does his name do now?"

Marisa spread her hands. "It will put these rumors to rest."

Her mother shook her head and pushed the rocker into motion with her foot. "No, it will not. There will always be those who believe something different."

"Then maybe I should have the test. Maybe that's the only way to stop people from gossiping."

"You know what people say I did for Andrew Easterling besides cooking and cleaning. The test will not stop those stories."

"Then what should I do? Tell me."

Her mother stared up at the mantle where a line of glass angels, her favorites, stood. "Have the test, *mi hija*. Then you will know."

Marisa felt suddenly adrift, not a new sensation this week. She knelt beside her mother's chair. "What are you saying, Mamá?"

"I am saying there is a part of your mind that will not take anyone's word who your father was, not even your Mamá's. Your mind wants to take the test. It is time."

Questions flooded Marisa's mind, but her mother was right. Her father's identity had been kept secret too long. She wasn't sure why she'd never considered a DNA test before, maybe because she'd been so sure Andrew Easterling wasn't her father. But with everything else that had happened this week, she was questioning all sureties in her life.

"All right, Mamá. I'll go tomorrow."

"I love you, *mi hija*. Please remember that."

"I'm always going to love you, Mamá. Who my father is won't change that."

On her way home, Marisa took the well-paved driveway instead of the shortcut path. She saw Scott Wentworth and his beautiful secretary through the downstairs windows. Scott held up a glass lamp and the secretary wrote on a clipboard.

Anger burned through her. He was cataloguing the Easterlings' possessions, deciding what he wanted for himself. It would serve him right to hold up his plans while they waited for her DNA test results. At that point, she knew for sure she would have the test.

An unexpected sob caught in her throat. Soon she'd know the truth about which man hadn't wanted her.

CHAPTER 10

Marisa overslept the next morning and woke with only minutes to spare before her first client would arrive. She called her mother's shop to tell her she was running late and to ask her to offer Mrs. Petosky some refreshments while she waited.

In the mirror, Marisa saw she looked like hell, having tossed and turned most of the night. There was no hope for it now. She'd have to meet her client and return home afterward.

She checked the steps carefully as she ran down them, holding onto the rail as she did. She wasn't going to risk another trip. Especially without Nick to catch her. Her cheeks burned as she remember the bulge she'd felt in his pants while she lay sprawled on top of him. Her lower body ached for him. She'd never ached for Kevin this way, yet she'd been his lover. Nick was a stranger, yet she couldn't stop thinking about him.

Shaking off her lusty thoughts, she started her car. At the end of her steep driveway, her brakes felt mushy. She made a mental note to have her car fluids checked. It was about time for an oil change.

But at the next cross street, the brakes didn't halt her increasing speed. She stomped the pedal to the floor as the car barreled down the hill toward the main intersection, but nothing happened. Cars drove by on the road below. God, what if she hit someone?

Her heart rate accelerated along with the car. Damn! If she were lucky, she'd fly through the intersection without hitting anyone. But then she'd hit the cars parked at the restaurant. She could try to turn on the main road, but at this speed, she'd probably lose control.

Oh God, there was no more time!

As soon as she hit Franklin Street, Marisa yanked the steering wheel to the right. The tires screamed as her car spun. Through the passenger side window, Marisa saw the blur of an approaching car. The other car's brakes shrieked. She jerked the steering wheel to the left to try to deflect away.

But her car didn't respond fast enough or turn far enough. The loud impact threw her against the door. There was a sharp pain in her head. Her car spun again, making her dizzy. As more brakes shrieked, she clung to consciousness and tried desperately to lessen the impact she knew was coming from the opposite side. The crash that hit the driver's side door rocked her entire body. Her head wobbled like a bobblehead. Then she lost the fight and everything went black.

*

Nick heard the crash through the open window of the sheriff's office where he'd gone to see Brian. He was on his feet when the second crash sounded, all his emergency training on high alert.

Brian scooped up his hat and fished his keys out of his pants pocket. "Nick, you're on leave."

Nick knew he wasn't supposed to use his paramedic training for another week, but he couldn't sit idly while someone might need his help. "I'm going." He followed Brian out to the squad car.

As they approached, Nick saw it was a bad one. One car was sandwiched between two others. They were going to need the Jaws of Life to . . .

"Son of a bitch! It's Marisa!" He flung himself out of the squad car before it stopped, his heart pumping hard, and sprinted to save her. Oh God, if anything happened to her . . . He couldn't bear to complete the thought.

He reached her car, skidding the last few feet. But the car that had hit the driver's side had crushed in the door. Through the window, he saw that Marisa's head lay on the steering wheel, her dark hair spread around her. She was so still that icy fear clutched him.

Nick tore around the car to the passenger's side. Luckily, the car that had hit that side hadn't stuck to Marisa's car or done as much damage, although the door was badly dented. He yanked on it with all his might again and again, her name pounding in his head as he pulled. He felt insane with frenzy to get to her. Finally he jerked it open.

Distantly he heard Brian shouting his name, but he only had eyes for Marisa. The airbag hadn't deployed because neither car had hit her head on.

He crawled across the shattered glass on the passenger seat to her. Then he was terrified to touch her. What if she'd been killed? For a moment, his sight blurred. But he had to know.

Swallowing, he reached out a wildly trembling hand. His pulse roared in his ears. God wouldn't take her from him like He'd taken Nick's father. He couldn't be that vindictive a God.

Nick's fingers touched Marisa's neck, but he couldn't feel anything. A sob rose in his throat. No! He moved his fingers an inch. There! Faint but steady. He felt a little lightheaded with relief and sagged against the seat.

"Nick! Nick!" Brian shouted nearly in his ear.

"She's alive." He couldn't believe how weak his voice sounded. "Thank God."

Nick reached for her seat belt release.

Brian grabbed his arm. "What are you doing?"

Nick shook Brian off. "I'm getting her out of here."

But Brian gripped his arm again and held on this time. "Nick, you don't know what kind of injuries she has. Let us get her out with the Jaws of Life and ascertain if she's hurt and, if so, how bad."

It was just like when his father died. His fellow firefighters had held him back then too. Nick felt wild as he struggled with Brian. "I can get her out. We don't need the Jaws." He was an EMT. It was his job to save people. He'd failed to save his father, but he wouldn't fail Marisa.

Brian got in his face. "Nick, you're not thinking straight. Let the professionals handle it."

"I *am* a professional."

"Not now you're not, buddy. Now you're the man who cares about this woman. Go wait with the spectators and let us do our jobs."

"I'm not leaving her." God no. He wasn't going anywhere until he knew she was all right.

Brian clamped his free hand on Nick's shoulder and forced him to turn around. "What are the symptoms of shock, Nick?"

Nick could hardly think of anything but Marisa. Slowly he repeated, as though by rote, "Weak, rapid pulse, confused and disoriented, rapid, shallow breathing, dilated pupils."

"Nick, you've got 'em. You're in shock."

He did feel disconnected, but right now, he only cared about one thing. "I'm not leaving her. Why don't you go help with the Jaws of Life?" Why didn't Brian understand how important this was to him?

Finally, Brian nodded and sighed. He released Nick's arm. "Okay, but don't get in the way."

"I can help."

"Not right now you can't."

Brian withdrew from the car. Nick hated feeling helpless. It was his job to help people, to save them. But ever since his dad had died, Nick had felt like he was losing more than he was saving. No matter how many hours he worked, he couldn't save enough of them. Now Marisa needed his help. He needed to be on the other side of the car yanking the door open.

No, he needed to be here holding her hand.

Nick snaked a hand to Marisa's neck again. Her wavy hair clung to him as he checked her pulse once more. It was stronger. He captured her hand and brought it to his mouth for a quick kiss.

The noises and voices outside the car rose and fell in a familiar, comfortable pattern. He'd worked hundreds of car accidents and knew the routine. He let the familiarity wash over him as Marisa's pulse beat under his hand. He watched the gentle rise and fall of her chest. Eventually, his breathing matched hers.

"Nick. Nick?" Brian shook him.

"Yeah? Her pulse is steady."

Brian thrust some material at him. "Nick, take these blankets and put one around her and the other around yourself."

"She's not cold. I'm not either."

"Your breathing is rapid and shallow, and she needs to be protected from the Jaws. Can you do this?" Brian spoke slowly like he was talking to a child.

"I'm not helpless."

Nick covered Marisa, using the action to probe gently for injuries. Not finding any obvious broken bones, he went back to breathing with her.

"Nick?" A woman's voice. "Nick?"

He turned his head to find Marisa's mother pale and wide-eyed. He gave a start to see so many people watching from a few feet away.

"Her pulse is steady."

"She will live?"

"I don't see any broken bones, Anjelita. I don't know if she's injured."

"She has never been in an accident before. All these bad things happening." She crossed herself.

Nick had thought the same thing; only it had begun with his dad's death. "I won't let her die." It was a stupid, rash promise he couldn't possibly keep, but he'd die trying.

Anjelita's eyes filled. "Thank you."

And just like that he felt like a hero, with nothing but a lie. But it hadn't felt like a lie. In fact, Marisa's pulse felt stronger under his fingers.

The noisy Jaws of Life halted further conversation. Finally, Marisa's door was opened. Nick leaped from his seat and barreled around the car.

"Nick!" Brian shouted.

But then Nick remembered how to be an EMT, how to protect an accident victim from further trauma, how to probe for injuries. As he worked alongside the Watkins Glen paramedics, Marisa groaned.

Her eyes fluttered open. "What happened?"

"You were in a car accident," Nick said. His legs trembled and he leaned against the car for support.

Her eyes flew to his. "The brakes wouldn't work. Oh my God, Nick, I couldn't stop the car!"

*

The Montour Falls ER staff poked, prodded, scanned and x-rayed Marisa for hours after the accident. Finally, they shook their heads, proclaimed it a miracle she hadn't received more than a bump on the head and numerous bruises, and cleared her to go home.

Throughout the ordeal, both Nick and her mother had stayed by her side. Her mother she understood, but Nick? There was a wild look in his eyes, not one she'd ever seen before, and one she couldn't name. He had a white bandage on his arm covering a deep scratch he didn't know how he got, but the blood stains on both of them told her it had happened in her car.

Now that she officially had calmed everyone's fears for her health, she realized where she was and what she had to do. It was as though fate had wanted to make sure she came here.

She swallowed and took hold of her mother's hand. "Mamá, it's time."

Anjelita frowned. "Time, *mi hija?*"

"For the test."

Her mother looked terrified for a moment, but then she nodded. "Yes."

"What test?" Nick straightened in his chair. "I thought the doctor cleared you."

"The DNA test. Remember, I'm supposed to have it done here."

"Oh." He glanced toward the nurse's station. "They'll be able to direct us."

In moments, she was whisked off to a lab where a very bright-eyed technician and a Middle Eastern man in a white lab jacket waited.

The man introduced himself as Dr. Ziad Smail. "The Watkins Glen lawyer briefed me. You can be assured I'll handle the test personally in the most expeditious manner possible."

Nerves fluttered in Marisa's stomach. This was it. She'd finally find out the answer she'd been waiting for.

"Whose DNA will you compare it to?" Nick asked.

Marisa's gaze jerked to him. That hadn't occurred to her. How would they track down the man who'd left town because her mother was pregnant?

"Watkins Glen is getting a court order to exhume Andrew Easterling's body."

"What!" Marisa exclaimed.

Her mother swooned, groaning, and Nick caught her, easing Anjelita gently into a chair. The technician brought smelling salts and waved it under Anjelita's nose until her mother pushed the young man away.

"Mamá, are you all right?"

"Poor Andrew! To defile his grave like that."

"There is another way." Everyone in the room looked at Nick. He took a deep breath and continued. "His daughter, Carolyn Wentworth, is in the morgue. You could test her."

"Oh, God." Marisa covered her mouth and closed her eyes, fighting off sickness.

"A half-sister?" Dr. Smail asked.

"Yes," Nick said.

"The father would be better, but we'll try. If it doesn't work, we can still exhume the body."

Anjelita moaned. Marisa felt sick again. She should have known they'd have to compare her results to someone already deceased, but to defile Carolyn that way . . . She shuddered.

"Open your mouth, Miss Avalos. This will only take a second."

A moment later, Dr. Smail whisked away with the swab clutched like a prize. And the DNA test was over except for the waiting.

"We'll call you with the results in a day or two." The young male technician smiled and left the room.

"In a way, I feel let down," Marisa said. "I guess I thought I'd know right away."

Nick took Anjelita's and her arm and led them out of the hospital.

"How are we going to get home?" Marisa asked.

They looked at one another. They'd ridden in the ambulance with her.

"Do they have cabs in this town?" Nick asked.

"No, but they have rental cars." The lawyer, Jantzen, detached himself from the side of the building. "I brought yours. I volunteered to play chauffeur for the woman who's going to save the town."

CHAPTER 11

Nick had the lawyer drop him at the sheriff's department. He didn't want to be separated from Marisa, but she had work to catch up on and he had something important to do.

As soon as he entered the building, he spotted Brian talking to Sheriff Kehr in the sheriff's office. He caught his friend's eye through the office window and Brian nodded. Nick waited at Brian's desk for the other conversation to end, tapping his foot with barely restrained anticipation.

Finally Brian joined him, settling into his desk chair with a sigh. "I heard Marisa is going to be fine."

Nick scooted to the edge of the other chair and leaned forward. "Yeah, the hospital proclaimed it a miracle. I think it had more to do with her trying to control her car after her brakes failed. It's terrifying to hear her tell the tale. What'd you find out about that, by the way?"

Brian frowned. "She had almost no brake fluid left. She probably went too long between oil changes."

"Were the other fluids low?"

Brian shook his head and shrugged. "We didn't check those."

"Last night Marisa tripped on a child's ball left on her stairs, but no children live in her building. I thought it was an accident, just neighbor children being careless. But after this morning, I'm not so sure."

"Who do you have in mind as the suspect?"

"I don't know. Does someone just want to scare Marisa, stop her from what she's doing, or does somebody want her silenced for good? She could easily have broken her neck on those tall, narrow stairs." A cold chill ran through Nick at the thought.

Brian lowered his voice and leaned forward. "You're talking about premeditated murder, Nick. I know you're burnt out from all the overtime you've been working. Is that affecting the way you look at things?"

Nick hadn't seen much goodness in the past six months, but he felt he was right about this. He shook his head. "I've been in town for two weeks, Bri. If it weren't so peaceful here, this place would be boring. But in the past four days a lot of things have happened. They can't be unrelated."

Brian sighed. "I can't think of anyone in town I'd believe capable of cold-blooded murder."

"It doesn't have to be a townsperson. What have you found out about Scott Wentworth?"

Brian gave Nick a sharp look. "His business is in debt, so, yeah, he's got a motive to push his wife in front of a train. Only why not just ask her for the money?"

"Most of her assets weren't liquid."

"She could have used them as collateral on a loan."

"I don't know, Brian. You're the cop, not me."

"I'll keep digging. But, Nick, even if he killed his wife—and I'm not saying he did—what reason would he have to come after Marisa?"

Nick kept an eye on the door to the sheriff's office. "The DNA test?"

"That didn't come up until last night." Brian, too, glanced at the other office and kept his voice low and flat.

"But the rumors have been here for years." Nick matched his friend's tone.

"A rumor isn't a motive for premeditated murder."

"There's bad blood between them."

Brian rolled his eyes. "Now that's a motive if you're in a gang. Scott Wentworth doesn't seem the type to get passionate about a grudge. In fact, I've always considered him to be cold."

"Marisa is in danger from someone. Two accidents in two days can't be coincidence, Brian." Nick felt desperate to convince his friend.

"We're just a small department, Nick. We can't spare someone to guard her." Brian looked thoughtful. "You're spending a lot of time with her. You could keep an eye on her."

"I'm not with her when she's at work, or when she goes home at night. What am I supposed to do, lurk in the bushes outside her apartment like a peeping Tom?" Nick's mind conjured a vision of her stripping while he watched. His cock hardened and he had to shift in his chair to get comfortable.

"Or maybe you want me to move in with her so I can ruin her reputation more than it is already."

Brian reached across the desk and gripped Nick's forearm. "You've fallen for her, man. I warned you that you were vulnerable. Are you in love with her?"

Nick scoffed. "I've known her for four days. How could I be in love with her?"

"I saw how you acted this morning. A man doesn't go crazy like that unless a woman means something to him. By the way, what happened to your arm?"

Nick lifted his forearm where the white bandage was prominent against his tanned skin. He'd pretty much forgotten about it. "I don't know."

"Do you remember yanking the passenger door open?"

"No." All he remembered was the desperate need to get to Marisa.

"That metal was pretty ragged."

"I don't remember. What does it matter anyway?" He'd done what he had to do. He'd do the same thing again if, God forbid, she were ever in a situation like that again.

"I think if it came down to a choice between Marisa's life and yours, you'd choose hers."

Nick thought it entirely possible, but he didn't say so. He hadn't analyzed what had been happening. He'd just been living it. And enjoying it, damn it.

"Nick, you're a hero. That's why you're so good at your job.

And right now Marisa needs a hero. But what happens when she doesn't need one anymore? In your current state, I'm afraid what would happen to you. Marisa won't mean to hurt you—she's a great woman—but she will. She's not ready for another relationship."

Nick gritted his teeth. "I know that." His timing couldn't suck any worse. Even if he gave Marisa six months or a year to get over her engagement, there'd be no guarantee a local man wouldn't catch her eye, or that she'd even be interested in Nick. After all, he wasn't local, she had no intention of moving, and he loved his job. He really wanted to go back to work.

"Then do yourself a favor and stay away from her," Brian said.

"I'll think about it."

Brian promised to do a little more digging into Scott Wentworth's background. By the time Nick left, he thought he'd convinced Brian that he wasn't imagining the danger to Marisa. He would have all the fluid levels in Marisa's car checked and call Nick with the findings.

Nick drove down to the docks so he could think about what Brian had said. If he wanted to return home heart whole, he'd walk away from Marisa now. He sat on the end of the Seneca Harbor Pier and watched the motorboats and sailboats dance gently on the dark waters of the lake. The scene was peaceful, the silence broken only by the slap of water against the wooden pier, by gulls wheeling overhead, and by voices carrying briefly across the docks. The sun baked his tight shoulders and made him glad to feel alive again.

The breeze off the deep water carried the chill of autumn. This warm spell wouldn't last; the seasons were changing. He felt restless inside, like he wanted to change too. But he didn't know in what way. All he knew was what he did best, and that was back in New York City.

When his cell phone rang several hours later and he heard Marisa's voice, he still didn't know what he should do. But he tried to heed Brian's advice.

"In all the excitement, I completely forgot my promise to take you places to photograph," she said.

"I understand. You're busy." Nick tried not to show encouragement in his voice.

"No, I mean yes, I am. But I've got to get away from these phone calls. People mean well and I know they care, but how many times am I expected to rehash the story?"

"You're a celebrity. It's the price of fame."

"I'd really like to see Eagle Cliff Falls. Would you go with me?" There was yearning in her voice.

Nick was weak. How could he say no to the things that made him feel alive? He crumbled. "When?"

"I'll pick you up in ten minutes. Can you be ready?" Excitement fueled her voice.

He was primed and ready to go. "Yeah. I'm sitting on the pier. I'll meet you in the parking lot."

"Great."

As he leaped to his feet and headed for the promenade, he knew he couldn't follow Brian's advice. Marisa needed him and what they shared together as much as he needed her. He'd heard it in her voice.

*

On the outskirts of the town of Montour Falls, Marisa drove through a campground sparsely populated with small trailers to the base of a hillside where a narrow stream flowed.

"Eagle Cliff Falls is up there?" Nick pointed up the hill. He couldn't imagine anything worthwhile being located in this place. The little campground looked sad and deserted.

"Yep." She almost smiled.

His breath caught and he waited, but her smile didn't bloom completely. They hadn't touched, not even accidentally. They hadn't made any gestures, either subtle or blatant, toward each other. Yet he could feel the tension throbbing between them.

They climbed the metal stairs up, up and up, twisting around the hillside following the stream to its source. So far there wasn't much to photograph. Nick could barely take his eyes off Marisa's satin hair and curvy butt.

Then the path turned left again and there were rapids on his right. Marisa waited beside him while he captured the power of the moving water in digital. But even photography couldn't calm him. He felt as tumultuous inside as the water. He might have lost Marisa today if her car had been hit harder or a different way. Her vivacity would have been snuffed out.

He wanted to grab her and hold her, press her life force to him to protect it and cherish it. Instead, he gripped the camera so hard he feared for its delicate metal parts.

She walked forward and the high close walls opened up into a small natural amphitheater. Nick stopped walking and stared, unable to even raise his camera. A thirty-foot waterfall splashed unhindered into the shallow pool below it. Most of the bottom of this canyon was a shallow pool. There was dry flat shale in front of him and another patch close to the falls. It was so magnificent and unexpected that words failed him.

He looked at Marisa to see if she realized how exceptional this place was. He read it in her eyes—she knew. Awareness zinged between them. They were alone together for the first time today.

Turning, she kicked off her shoes and strolled into the water. Nick lifted his camera and captured her against the grandeur of the canyon and the falls. He filmed the way the water droplets flew around her and clung to her shapely calves she walked. She stopped on the dry shale and turned to him. The heat in her eyes nearly singed him. His cock came to immediate life. She lifted her hands to the hem of her shirt and slowly, slowly she pulled it up.

Nick's mouth dried. He pressed the shutter automatically, capturing the act on film. Her lacy cream bra was sexier than anything advertised by supermodels on TV. As she pulled her shirt over her head, her dark curls tumbled free. His breath stopped. She tossed the shirt away.

She lowered her hands to the fly of her shorts. The snap came open, displaying a V of light brown flesh. She slid the zip down and then wiggled so suggestively Nick's hard-on got harder.

The shorts dropped and Marisa kicked them away. She did a slow pirouette in her bra and panties, posing for the camera. He couldn't believe she'd allow him to take such private photographs. He began to sweat.

She reached behind her and unsnapped her bra. The straps slid from her shoulders. For a moment, she stared into the camera, holding onto the bra, and then the cups slipped down her breasts uncovering her dark nipples. Nick yearned to suck them. He photographed their lush beauty instead, loving them with the lens instead of his hands.

Slowly, she lowered the V-shaped lacy panties that matched her bra. First, a thatch of black curls was revealed, and then shadows between her thighs where her pleasure hid. Nick still photographed what was the most erotic act he'd ever witnessed even though he wanted desperately to explore the secrets she'd exposed.

Raising her arms, she lifted her hair from her shoulders. God, he wanted her. With every fiber of his being he wanted her. Why was she tempting him this way?

He photographed all of it, the wanton striptease, the come-hither look, the heated desire in her eyes, the puckered nipples, and flushed face that spoke her desire better than words.

Then she stepped backward until the waterfall hit her, splashing her shoulders, chest, nipples, belly, thighs, and calves—all the places he wanted to lick. She looked at him and he knew she wanted him to lick them too.

He had enough sense to set the camera down on a ledge. He had enough appreciation to wish he'd brought a tripod so he could film what they were about to do. And he had enough intelligence to leave his clothes on the dry shale and sheath himself with his only condom before he went to her. And then he was lost.

CHAPTER 12

The water felt cold on Marisa's bare body, but Nick's hands burned when he captured her. She'd wanted him to come to her, had tempted him beyond a point she knew he could resist, but she still felt a thrill when he touched her. He lifted her easily until her breasts were level with his mouth. He clamped his lips around her nipple and sucked hard with his hot mouth. She cried out as pleasure streaked directly to her womb. Her vagina moistened and clenched.

He sucked her other breast just as hard, his mouth burning hot against her cooled flesh. She arched her back, pressing more of her breast deeper into his mouth. She was on fire.

She wriggled against him as he suckled one breast and then the other. Slowly he slid her down his body until she was astride his hard, hot cock. It burned her vulva with a seductive heat. Still, he bent over her chest and feasted on her breasts. She rubbed her slick flesh against his burning hot erection.

Nick groaned and raised his head. His short hair was plastered to his scalp. "This is going to happen. If you don't want it, stop me now." His voice was a deep growl.

"I want it." She'd never wanted anything this much. She clutched at his biceps.

"I didn't intend to seduce you."

"You're not the one doing the seducing."

His expression was wild, carnal, violent. "If someone shows up, I won't stop. Once you say yes, nothing is going to stop me until we've both come."

"I want it. I want you."

"I'm not your nice fiancé. I can't be gentle. Not this time." There was a hard edge to his words.

"I don't want gentle and I don't want Kevin." She realized the truth of her words with a pang of regret, quickly suppressed. She wanted this man and this mating.

He kissed her hard and quick. She wanted more.

But Nick growled, "Hold on." He lifted her over his cock and with one powerful thrust entered her completely. They both groaned aloud.

"Oh God," he panted. "You feel good."

"More!" She needed his heat.

He lifted her and shoved home again. Flames licked through her lower body. Again and again he pulled her down onto his thick penis. But it wasn't enough.

"Harder!" She needed to be fused to him.

Nick gripped her to him, the world spun and suddenly she felt cool stone against her back. She barely had a moment to register their changed position before Nick plunged into her. Marisa cried out, bucking up against him with the pleasure. She'd never been filled so well before. Nick grabbed her ankles and lifted them onto his shoulders, pressing in against her so that she was spread wide.

And then he plunged. Marisa screamed, the sound echoing off the rock walls. Contractions ripped through her vagina. Nick rode her hard through them. It was an inferno of pleasure so intense she could barely catch her breath.

She tried to move with him but then another orgasm tore through her. She pressed her heels into his back, her toes curling, as he moved forcefully inside her body. His breathing sounded ragged.

"Once more and I come with you."

"Do it!"

Nick was strong. His thrusts raised her body as he plunged deeply into her. He slid his hands under her buttocks and lifted. The next thrust was so hard and deep it stole her breath. The next stole her vision as her orgasm began. The third stole all thought but screaming pleasure.

Marisa combusted. She melted into him. He melted into her. Fused. Became one.

Cooled. Nick lay gasping on her, his cock still jerking with his orgasm. Little tongues of flame still licked at her clitoris, making aftershocks ripple through her vagina.

She'd never had an experience like this before. She'd heard about it, but assumed she was one of those women who didn't enjoy sex.

She'd been dead wrong. She enjoyed sex all right—with Nick. Mamá had been right about him. His touch set her body aflame. Did she do the same for him?

Marisa gripped him tight to her. What if he was the only man she could experience this with? What if these few days were the only time in her life when a man would make her burn with desire?

"Can we do it again?" she whispered into his ear.

Nick huffed a laugh, his body jiggling hers intimately. More aftershocks rippled through her body and she clenched around his penis in response.

"Please."

He lifted his head. The lines of strain in his face were gone. There was a light in his eyes she'd never seen before.

"You nearly killed me that time."

"I want to do it again."

"I don't have any more condoms."

She hesitated. She was a responsible adult. She could raise a child as a single mother like her mother had done, but she knew there were other risks.

"I'm clean. Are you?"

"Yes, but I wouldn't take any risk with you. If you want me, I'm willing, but not without a condom."

"I want you. Your place or mine?"

"Mine. There's more privacy for you to scream."

"Will I scream?"

He thrust into her and she gasped. He was hard again.

"Most definitely."

Marisa gripped his forearms. It was all or nothing. "Nick, I want you to do everything to me."

He ran a gentle palm over the bruise on her bicep. "Everything? You're sure?"

"Yes. Don't hold anything back. I want to experience it all with you."

"That'll take at least all night."

"I'm willing." More than willing.

He kissed her, a promise of more to come. "Then we'd better get dressed. It's going to be a long ride home."

*

The crash of thunder jerked Nick from an exhausted doze. For a moment, he didn't know where he was. The next instant a bright flash lit up the bedroom, illuminating the Latina goddess in his bed. Marisa. He didn't think it was possible, but he began to grow hard again. They'd made love all afternoon, evening and long into the night. As promised, he'd taken her in every room, in every position and given her an orgasm every way he knew how. His lips had tasted every part of that luscious body and hers had tasted his. She'd done things to him he didn't think a woman would do. She'd made him come in so many ways. But apparently he had one more romp in him.

Thunder crashed again, rattling the walls.

"Kevin?"

Nick froze. His heart quit beating. He couldn't breathe. And then he could breathe again and it hurt. She wasn't his. This was temporary, until he returned home. She was still in love with another man.

Damn, damn and damn. He'd never had a night like this, never had a partner like her, never been fused to a woman as he'd been to Marisa. But she wasn't his.

When the lightning flashed, she was sitting up in bed, naked and so lovely it hurt to look at her. "Nick?"

"I'm here."

"I was dreaming."

"It's just a storm."

"What's the matter?" She reached a hand toward him.

Nick took hold of it. "Nothing. I just wish we had more time." Time enough for her to fall out of love with Kevin and then what? What did he want with more time?

Marisa tugged him down next to her. Her nipples were peaked and they pressed into his chest. His arousal, which had disappeared after she called her fiancé's name, came to life again. He ran a hand across her nipples, loving the feel of them.

She sucked in her breath. "Again?"

"I'm working on it." He pinched her nipples lightly.

Marisa's breathing deepened. "I could help."

"You will help. It's just going to take a while this time."

"That sounds interesting." Her voice was a sexy come-on.

"I'm not going to stop, even if you cry uncle."

"I don't want my uncle. I want you."

Nick swallowed. If only that were true beyond what they were doing in bed. "Are you sure you want me? I've thought of something I haven't done to you yet, but it involves bondage."

"Really?" She drew out the word.

"And a little something in my luggage I haven't introduced you to."

"Will I like it?"

"It'll make you scream."

Marisa held her wrists out to him. "Tie me up."

*

Marisa lay on her side and listened to Nick whistle as he made coffee in the kitchen. It was past time to get up and go to work, but she didn't think she could move. She didn't know how Nick walked straight this morning, especially after that last romp. Well, actually, her body had taken the majority of the action. Thinking about what he'd done to her made her clitoris tingle and her vagina clench. She pressed her thighs together. God, she was going to have to have sex with him this morning to slake her post orgasm pre-orgasm.

He was so imaginative. She hadn't known that particular item could be used like that. Her clitoris tingled again. Damn it, she was insatiable for him.

So this was what man-woman relations were supposed to be like. No fumbling, no lukewarm passion, no peck on the cheek afterward. Adults felt real passion. They craved to make their partner scream in every way. They hungered for their partner's touch over and over and over.

She'd had none of that with Kevin. She'd spent eight years waiting for him. Sure, she'd pined for his company, but not for his touch. Already she craved Nick's touch. She counted the seconds until he was back in her bed again and in her body.

Marisa couldn't imagine what she'd do after he returned home again—and he would. His leave was almost up and he was desperate to return to work. He'd told her he didn't want to hurt her. She'd told him the same thing.

But now she knew he would hurt her. This craving she felt for him was so much more than physical. It couldn't be love—it was too soon for that—but this was no one night stand. She liked him a lot. She could even imagine living and loving with him for the rest of her life. If only they had time to build a relationship that would last.

She'd had eight years to build such a relationship with Kevin, but they hadn't. Was it possible to forge bonds with Nick in the short time they had left? The heat between them was hot enough to fuse. Where Kevin had been a sparkler that sputtered out, Nick was a raging forest fire that consumed everything in its path—including her—until she was part of the flames.

She'd seen the pain in his hollow eyes and had wanted to give him the joy of life again. But he'd given her the same and much more. It was like her mother and father all over again. There would never be another man like Nick for her. How could anyone else measure up?

Nick walked into the room holding two cups of steaming fragrant coffee. He looked very sexy naked. "I brought you something."

"It had better be from your luggage. I'm halfway to an orgasm and I just need a little help getting there."

He lifted one dark eyebrow. Part of a dimple showed in his cheek. "I only have what you can see. But I think I know what will help."

"God, I hope so." She pressed her thighs together harder.

He placed the coffee cups on the dresser and climbed into bed behind her. His hot skin singed her where they touched.

"Do I have your permission to do whatever it takes to achieve your goal?"

"God, yes!"

"You're so easy."

CHAPTER 13

Later that morning Marisa let her lover drive her home. It was only a few miles from his cabin to her apartment and it was late enough that the other tenants in her building would already be at work, so they wouldn't see her coming home dressed in yesterday's clothes. In a small town, it was all about rumor control.

As they approached the pier, Nick stopped the car. She glanced to the left to see what had caught his attention. What looked like all the town's police vehicles were parked in the lot.

"What's going on?" she asked.

"We'd better find out." He pulled into an empty parking space.

She'd noticed Nick seemed to be attracted to trouble spots. Occupational hazard for a firefighter, she supposed. Maybe like a cop, he couldn't turn it off. She wondered how that had added up to job burnout.

They had to cross the railroad tracks where Carolyn had died only a few days ago. Marisa felt chilled to the bone, as though Carolyn's ghost haunted the place where she'd died. Maybe Carolyn couldn't rest until Marisa proved she hadn't killed herself. Guilt pressed in on her. While she'd been burning up the sheets in Nick's bed, thinking only of pleasure, Carolyn's name remained slandered. Marisa hurried down the promenade, as though she could outrun the guilt.

They found Brian on the pier looking harried, his hair in complete disarray. When he saw them, he groaned and rubbed his forehead.

"What happened?" Nick demanded.

"We've got a lot of dead fish and an extremely high salt level in the lake this morning."

"More sabotage?" Nick asked.

"It could have been the storm."

"What storm?" Marisa could have kicked herself.

Brian pinned her with his gaze. "The one last night that knocked down tree limbs, took off half the fall foliage, and left part of the town without power. Don't tell me you slept through it?"

Marisa vaguely remembered her screams of pleasure vying with the ferocity of a storm. Her cheeks burned.

Brian's glance traversed between her and Nick. His eyes widened and then he narrowed them at Nick. "I see." He studied her again and she squirmed under his examination. She'd showered with Nick—twice—but her clothes from yesterday were dirty and wrinkled, and her lips were slightly swollen from hours of kissing. She looked like what she was—a woman who'd spent the night in a man's bed.

Brian looked out toward the lake, frowning. "I've sent out divers again to look for man-made causes. We're checking the salt levels along this end of the lake. The sheriff's got me handling the fishermen, who are pretty upset, and gathering reports as they come in. We've even had calls from property owners on the west side of the lake about fish on their beaches. The inns are pretty concerned."

"Is there a tie-in with what we talked about yesterday?" Nick asked.

"Too soon to tell." A small boat containing two men chugged for the pier. "Listen, I have to talk to these fishermen. I'll let you know what we find out."

Nick nodded and took hold of Marisa's arm. She fought the urge to slide her hand upward and interlace her fingers with his.

"Nick, Marisa, be careful." Brian stared hard at Nick.

As they made their way back to the rental car, Marisa spoke her confusion aloud. "What'd Brian mean by that?"

"There are a lot of odd things happening. We have to be aware of what's going on around us, of who is around us."

"Does he think the problems with the plant are related to my problems?"

"He doesn't know yet. But keep alert for things you think are accidents that might not be."

Her head snapped up. "You don't think my car accident was an accident?"

"No."

"What else don't you think was an accident?"

"Your trip on the stairs."

Marisa's belly went cold. "And you think they weren't accidents because of the trouble at the plant?"

"I don't know."

Nick settled her in the car and they drove the short distance up the hill to her apartment. She waited until they were inside to broach another subject.

"Your friend knows we spent the night together." Her cheeks burned, even though she willed them not to.

"He's a trained observer."

She led the way into her bedroom, her body abuzz with the knowledge of where they were. Did he think she'd brought him in here for more of what they'd shared last night? When she turned, her eyes met his. His were heated chocolate—a marvelous idea with lots of possibilities.

"What are you thinking?" he asked.

"Melted chocolate, you and me naked." Her lower body tingled.

He groaned. "You're going to be the death of me. I'm willing but I don't know if I'm able just yet. How about a raincheck until tonight?"

Excitement sizzled through her veins. He wanted to spend another night with her. He was dark, virile strength amid the flowered femininity of her bedroom. He was a flame that burned away the memory of any other presence. She wanted him to imprint himself on her pale sheets and on her tanned flesh.

"Or this afternoon?" She didn't think she could wait until dark.

"Yeah, that might work."

Marisa swallowed. "I have to change clothes."

"I'll watch." He settled himself in the room's overstuffed chair.

Marisa hesitated. She didn't have yesterday's near-death experience driving her to feel alive again. No, she had the memories of every moment they'd shared, every intimacy. Nick was no stranger to her body and she fully intended to share it with him again.

She lifted her shirt, peeling it slowly off her body, and then pulling it over her head in a rush. She didn't want to miss a moment of Nick's intent expression. Tossing her shirt aside, she unsnapped her shorts. As she pulled down the zipper, the heat of Nick's desire seared her, branding her flesh.

Wriggling out of her shorts reminded her of yesterday. She saw the memories in Nick's dark eyes. She wanted to repeat yesterday, everything they'd done together. She licked her dry lips.

Her bra came off easier than it had yesterday. Now she had no doubts about offering her breasts for his mouth to worship. She shimmied out of her panties in a rush. She couldn't wait to spread her legs and let Nick feast on what was between them. Her vagina clenched in anticipation.

"God, you're beautiful and so sexy." Nick's voice sounded like a hungry growl.

His words flowed over her like hot syrup. Her nipples stood at attention. Her clitoris tingled.

"I should have had protein for breakfast," he muttered.

Marisa couldn't help the disappointment she felt.

"But how about a little snack? Come here, honey."

Her lower body clenched. She tried to be seductive as she walked toward him, but her legs trembled badly.

Nick ran his palms up her thighs and around to caress her buttocks and then her back. Marisa shivered with desire.

"You know I want you, right?" His voice sounded thick.

She knew by the fire in his eyes he was telling the truth. She nodded.

"I'd spend all day in bed making love to you if I could. I should have paced myself last night." He continued to caress up and down her body, moving inwards on her thighs. She was very wet for him.

"But I wanted you so badly." He stroked her lower lips.

Marisa shuddered. Her nipples ached. Her vagina clenched.

When he looked up at her, his eyes were molten darkness. "You like that. You like everything I do to you." He slid a finger across her channel.

"Yes. Everything."

Nick pushed his finger into her. She clenched around it, moaning. He pulled it out and stroked across her clitoris with his wet finger. Her body quivered.

"You can't scream here. No matter how good it feels." He stroked again once, twice.

Marisa stiffened, her clitoris throbbing and her vagina aching.

Nick pushed her backwards as he rose from the chair, stroking a wet finger across one hardened nipple. Marisa moaned. He pressed her into the chair he'd just vacated and pulled her hips forward. Then he knelt between her legs and smoothed her thighs wide open.

"You can't scream."

She watched his dark head lower between her thighs. She tensed in anticipation, clenching hard inside. The first touch of his tongue on her clitoris made her jerk. A jolt of pleasure ached through her core. She arched to his tongue. He pressed hard, stroking. Marisa groaned. Her vagina clenched on emptiness.

"Don't scream." His words blew across her sensitized flesh.

He spread her vulva wide with his thumb and forefinger and speared her clitoris with his tongue. Marisa stuck her fist in her mouth, strangling a shriek.

His tongue stroked flame across her clitoris over and over. The pleasure built higher and higher until she feared she'd combust. Yet she never wanted it to end. She wriggled away from the intensity of his touch, but he followed, pressing the most sensitive spot. He pushed two fingers into her vagina. Marisa bucked, which pressed her against his mouth. She was almost there. He pushed in a third finger, thrusting fast. His tongue stroked hard.

Orgasm grabbed her. She convulsed helplessly under the dual

assaults of pleasure. He wouldn't stop. She cried out against her fist. He intensified his assaults. It was too much, too much. He forced her into orgasm again, and she bucked hard against his mouth.

Then he let her rest. Her vagina tightened over and over with aftershocks. He crawled up her lax body and placed his hot lips around her nipple, sucking. Marisa squirmed under him, groaning against her fist. Her vagina clenched again.

He sucked her other breast, making savoring noises. She squirmed against him and reached for his shorts.

But he stopped her, gripping her hands.

She stared a question at him. He leaned forward and fused his mouth to hers. He tasted of her. She ate him up, his warm, wonderful lips.

Finally he pulled away, gasping. "That's to hold you over until later."

"But you . . . " How could he not finish what they'd started? How could he take nothing for himself when she was willing to give him anything he wanted?

"I'd come inside you if I could, but . . . " He looked sheepish. "Even after all that, my guy is still tired."

Marisa laughed, as she knew he'd intended. The tension lessened. "But, I want you all night."

"I'll be up for it—literally—by this afternoon, I promise. You'll get all night. And just to make sure, I'll stop at the drugstore and buy something to help."

"You don't need the blue pill." Just the opposite.

"Not a pill." He kissed her. "They sell something to help sustain an erection for hours. And it comes with a little added pleasure for a man's partner."

Marisa didn't want to ask how he knew about the product, or whom he might have used it with. She burned with jealousy. But reality intruded. Nick lived in New York City. He was going back there, to the women who lived there. She had only a few more days with him.

"Buy a gross of them."

*

Marisa was glad Nick was along as she climbed the steps of the big white house to face Scott Wentworth for the first time since the lawyer's office. She was afraid she'd scream like a banshee or lunge for Scott's face with her fingernails for cataloguing his wife's family's belongings like a shopkeeper.

It took a long time before the front door opened. And there stood Brooke Shroyer, her long blonde hair in disarray around her shoulders, wearing only a man's shirt, which covered her to mid-thigh. She had legs a mile long. She looked shocked to see them.

Words failed Marisa, but not Brooke. "Scott, someone to see you," she called over her shoulders, making the word "someone" sound like an insult. Then she slinked away.

Marisa didn't dare look at Nick. Her thoughts and emotions collided together like the train cars had the day Carolyn was killed.

Scott appeared in the doorway, shirtless, with his belt undone and his always-controlled hair rumpled. Marisa couldn't believe what she was seeing.

He looked from her to Nick, his expression icy, and sneered, "You've got some nerve coming here."

"Me?" Marisa wanted to scream at him and hit him. Or scratch his eyes out and bite him. Her anger seethed inside her on a primal level.

But Scott lashed out first. "You claimed you were my wife's friend, but as soon as she's dead you try for her fortune with your vicious lies."

"I'm not the liar."

But Scott wasn't finished. "You've decided to use the rumors of your bastard origins to your advantage. What's that make you?"

She wasn't the one who was disloyal. "At least I'm not counting her pennies while she's lying in the morgue." Marisa choked on the words. "And screwing your secretary in her bed!"

"A man has needs, Miss Avalos. No man will begrudge me solace while I'm in mourning, and Miss Shroyer is willing."

"You're despicable!" Marisa fought tears. Poor Carolyn, married to this . . . snake . . . for four long years. He couldn't have loved her, not when he moved on to the next warm body without a second thought. She'd been right not to like him.

She glared him down. "I want the box of mementos Carolyn left me in her will."

Scott narrowed his eyes, and his expression went even colder. "I haven't had time to look for it."

Of course he hadn't. He'd been too busy with his money and his secretary to give a thought for anybody else. "I don't care. I want it. Let me in and I'll look for it myself."

"I think you'd better let her in, Wentworth." A hint of menace laced Nick's words. He'd been so silent Marisa had nearly forgotten he was there.

Scott studied Nick's dark face and with a surly look opened the door wider and led the way down the hall to Mr. Easterling's office. Each room they passed contained chaos, like a tornado had blown through the house. It was the same in the office. Everything was out of its usual place, clustered in jumbled piles. Mr. Easterling had been a tidy man and his office had been a place of organized busyness. He would turn in his grave if he saw this mess.

And Marisa's mother never would have tolerated such disorder in this house. She prided herself on her excellent housekeeping.

Marisa burned with impotent rage. Legally she could do nothing to stop Scott, not until the lawyer got an injunction. In the meantime, she fought tears. She had to be strong in front of Scott. She had a feeling he'd savor her pain if he knew how badly he was hurting her.

"It's supposed to be in here." Scott leaned against the office doorjamb.

There were piles of paper everywhere. Clearly, Scott had been busy determining the extent of his new business empire. Marisa didn't know how she would find anything in here, but it took only moments to locate the box sitting on the floor close to the desk. It had been opened.

Why had Scott claimed he hadn't had time to look for it, when clearly he'd found it? Marisa glanced inside the 2-by-2 cardboard box. She would have no way of knowing if he'd removed anything he didn't want her to have.

Closing the flaps, Marisa stormed to the door with Nick following.

"Don't think your ploys will stop me for long, Miss Avalos." Scott's eyes narrowed. "As soon as that test proves your slut of a mother can't name your father, I'll be selling everything."

Rage burned hot in Marisa. Her fists clenched around the box.

But Nick's voice cut like glass. "Shut your mouth, Wentworth, or I'll shut it for you."

Marisa would have chosen the latter, but Nick propelled her out the front door.

"I knew there was a reason you brought your cop bodyguard with you." Scott slammed the door shut.

Marisa fumed. The bastard. How dare he say such things about her mother.

Nick took the box from her and headed down the steps. She stood on the wide wooden porch without moving while anger seethed inside her like storm-tossed seas. She didn't want to leave. Her fists clenched and her arm muscles tightened. She wanted to go back in there and bloody Scott's nose.

"Marisa." Nick's gentle, understanding voice drew her attention. The sympathy in his dark eyes was a balm on her roiling soul. With just a look, he lured her down the steps to his side.

He stroked a free hand over her hair and his simple action unlocked her throat. "He's ruining all the wonderful memories I have of this place."

"I'm sorry." He spoke with quiet, sincere sympathy.

Her anger flared again, but not at him. "You're not the one who needs to apologize."

"I know." He slid the box into the opened trunk and slammed it shut. "Why don't you show me around the place and tell me a little about your life here. Let's thumb our noses at Wentworth with a tour."

Her smile of gratitude felt strained. But he took her hand and they walked slowly around the huge house, which was part gray brick and part white wood. It had been far too large for one small family of three, even if they were the richest in town. But Marisa and her mother had shared it with the Easterlings for twenty-five years. Her life had been wrapped up in this house.

This might be one of the last times she could wander the grounds. Everything was changing, including her. She had no idea what the result would be. This week she'd been severed from everything she'd known in her youth and thrust into the unknown. She'd been frightened in this new reality, but not everything in it was terrible.

Marisa glanced at the man beside her. He wasn't part of her youth; he was part of her maturity. She'd discovered things being with him that she hadn't known, about herself and about the world she now inhabited. She felt more alive with him than she'd ever felt before, and that was unsettling to learn.

She shared the stories of her childhood with Nick as they strolled the grounds, to bridge the two halves of her life. She described how she and Carolyn had played hide and seek in that cellar, how Mr. Easterling taught them to skate on the cement veranda, how the many flower gardens, now gone to seed, had been planted for Mrs. Easterling's enjoyment.

"She didn't go outside?" Nick asked.

"Not much. Her wheelchair was hard to push across the grass. She looked at her flowers from the windows."

"So she was a prisoner of this house."

"Oh no. Mr. Easterling took her on trips. She loved to travel, but she'd sleep a lot when she got home. Mamá always worked twice as hard at the house after they returned from a trip. She'd come home exhausted."

Brian Nash had been right about the ferocity of last night's storm. Twigs and branches littered the lawn and lots of leaves had blown down. The mature trees were now half bare of their beautiful autumn colors. As they approached the hexagonal pool and fountain in the side yard, Marisa saw it was covered with leaves. At the moment, clouds blocked the sun, making the pond appear neglected.

"Someone should clean out the pond. I always loved it when the fountains poured water into it during the summer. Carolyn and I played here a lot." The iron benches at the edges of the garden had not yet been put away for the winter. Marisa wondered who would do that chore now.

As the sun broke through the clouds, she heard Nick draw in breath. "Marisa." He grabbed her arm and yanked her away from the pond.

But not before she'd seen the woman floating in it.

CHAPTER 14

"Oh my God! Is she dead?" Marisa cried.

Nick knew live women didn't float face down in the water. He had to protect Marisa from further trauma. "Stay here and call 911 while I check it out." Once again, he slipped effortlessly into his emergency training.

As Marisa pulled her cell phone out of her purse, Nick returned to the pond. Had the sun not come out at that moment, he and Marisa might have passed right by without noticing the body. From the leaves covering her, the woman had obviously been in the water since last night's storm.

The water was no more than two feet deep, so he reached out and gripped the woman's wrist. It was cold. He held on for half a minute, but felt no pulse. Tugging the body toward him, he tried to get a neck pulse. But she was long gone.

"Is she dead?"

"Yeah." Poor woman. What was she doing in a pond on the Easterling grounds? Had she drowned as a result of the storm? And how had she drowned in such shallow water? He had plenty of questions, but no answers. It made him uneasy that the woman had died here.

Marisa moved closer. "The sheriff's coming."

"Damn it, Marisa. I told you to stay back." His uneasiness lent his voice an edge. He winced hearing it. He hadn't meant to snap at her.

"Who is it?" Her question sounded strained.

Damn, he'd hurt her. "I don't know. I haven't turned her over. Please go back over there." He pointed to the iron benches at the edge of the garden. "You don't need to see this." He needed to do his job and protect her, but in order to do both, she had to move farther away.

Nick tuned out Marisa's grumbling about bossy men. At another, less crucial time, it might have made him smile. He studied the dead woman. From the back, with her long dark hair, she looked like Marisa.

Cold dread gripped him. Had someone mistaken this woman for Marisa in the dark and caused her to have a fatal accident? If that was so, he had to be careful not to disturb any evidence. Slowly he turned the woman face up. The face was slightly bloated from being in the water, but he didn't recognize her.

Marisa's gasp came from right over his shoulder.

His voice came out sharper than he intended. "Damn it, Marisa, don't you listen?"

"You're not my father." She gripped his bicep. "It's Elizabeth Hernandez. She's fairly new to town. Her husband works at the plant. What was she doing here?"

Nick didn't think it a coincidence that a Latina woman was dead. He heard the sirens coming up the hill and pulled Marisa back from the pond. She was shivering, so he wrapped his arm around her and pulled her tight against him. She snuggled into him.

"What was she doing here?" Marisa repeated.

Nick wanted to know the same thing. "I don't know. Was she the housekeeper?"

"No. That was Mamá's job until the Easterlings were killed. Carolyn didn't have a housekeeper. The only people who worked here were the grounds-keeping service she hired to take care of the estate."

"Maybe she works for them."

Marisa shook her head against his chest. "I don't think so."

Brakes squealed, car doors slammed, and many footsteps and voices headed their way. Sheriff Kehr was the first one around the side of the house and Nick prepared to deal with the fool. But Brian followed right behind the sheriff, and Nick relaxed. No matter how misguided the sheriff might be regarding Scott Wentworth, Brian would seek the truth.

Suddenly Nick realized how close they were to Wentworth. It couldn't be a coincidence. He had to get Brian away from the sheriff so they could talk.

Brian nodded at them before proceeding to the pond. The volunteer paramedics followed him.

"It's Elizabeth Hernandez," Marisa said.

"Eddie Hernandez is going to be heartbroken," one of the paramedics said.

Brian signaled Nick and Marisa closer. "Is this the way you found her?"

Nick told Brian everything they knew. The deputy frowned, but before they could discuss anything further, a loud voice interrupted.

"What the hell's going on here?" Scott Wentworth stalked around the side of the house. He looked like he'd just finished another tryst with his secretary. His mouth was swollen and his hair tousled.

Nick felt Marisa stiffen in his arms, and he held her tighter.

Sheriff Kehr hurried to Scott. "Mr. Wentworth, a young woman was found drowned in your pond."

"Drowned?" Scott said. "What woman?"

"Elizabeth Hernandez."

Scott shook his head and held up his hands. "I don't know anyone by that name. What was she doing on my property?"

"We don't know that yet, Mr. Wentworth." The sheriff practically bowed and scraped to Scott.

During the rest of the sheriff's exchange, Nick took Brian aside, but kept an eye on Marisa. "The woman was Latina. She was on the Easterling estate, where Marisa often walks home from visiting her mother. I think someone might have mistaken her for Marisa."

Brian's breath whooshed out. "Jesus. You think it was Wentworth?"

Nick glanced over at Scott. "He's putting on an Oscar-worthy performance. You should ask for his alibi."

Brian glanced in that direction, too. "With Sheriff Kehr here?"

Nick lowered his voice. "If Wentworth is a killer, Sheriff Kehr isn't going to win another term in office."

"But he can fire or demote me while he's still sheriff."

"Two women are dead under mysterious circumstances, Brian. Another has had a string of near-fatal accidents. Aren't you concerned about the women in this town?"

Brian jerked back and his face suffused with red. "Of course I am. Wait here and I'll ask."

Brian returned to where the sheriff was still talking to Wentworth. "Excuse me, Mr. Wentworth, but since this is your property, I'd like to know your whereabouts during the past twelve hours."

"Deputy, I'm sure that's not necessary." Sheriff Kehr was making denying motions with his hands.

Brian stood straighter. "Sir, if he was any other person and we found a dead woman on his property, we'd demand an accounting of his whereabouts."

"It's all right, Sheriff," Scott soothed. "I've been here since about nine last night doing an inventory of my property."

"Can anyone vouch for that?" Brian asked.

"My secretary, Brooke Shroyer."

"What time did she go to bed?"

Scott's smile was smug. "The same time I did, and in the same bed. My faithful secretary knows I'm in pain and she considerately has offered me comfort in my darkest hours."

"She can account for your whereabouts all night?"

"All night. She helped me relax enough to fall asleep. When the storm woke me, I realized my wife wasn't there and would never be there again, and Brooke took my mind off Carolyn for the next several hours." The last words carried all kinds of intimations.

Nick saw Marisa's cheeks darken. Her hands were clenched. He moved toward her.

"I'll need to verify that with your secretary," Brian said.

"Fine. Come with me." Scott wheeled and headed back the way he'd come.

Brian followed Wentworth around the house.

Nick felt this was an excellent time to remove Marisa from the scene. "Sheriff, may we leave now? We've given our statements to Deputy Nash. Miss Avalos has had a traumatic week and seeing another dead body isn't helping any."

"Yes, you're free to go." He sounded eager to be rid of them and turned back to the paramedics.

Nick hurried Marisa the shortest route to the car. She offered no resistance, so he was certain she wanted distance between her and Scott Wentworth.

"Where are we going?" she asked as he started the car.

"My place or yours, you pick." He put the car in gear and started down the long driveway.

"I need to see my mother and tell her what's happened."

"Not yet." He made a snap decision. "I guess we'll go to your apartment." He pulled out onto the road and turned left.

"Why not yet?"

"There's something we need to discuss about what we saw today, in private."

As Marisa opened her mouth, Nick pulled into her driveway, so she held her questions.

After they had the apartment door closed, Marisa turned to him. "What did we see?"

Nick decided bluntness was called for in this situation. "That was no recent affair between Wentworth and his secretary. She wasn't a woman comforting a recent widower."

Marisa's hand flew to her mouth. "Oh my God. He was cheating on Carolyn." She sank into a chintz living room chair.

Nick sat on the couch next to her. "It's either another motive to get rid of his wife, or . . ." He didn't want to force the knowledge on Marisa.

"Or what? What's worse than murdering his wife to make room for his mistress?"

Nick was going to have to be the bearer of bad news. His muscles tightened. He hated what he had to do, but it had to be faced. "Could your friend have found out about her husband's affair and killed herself?"

*

Marisa felt shocked, and then outraged. She sprang from her chair. "I told you she didn't kill herself!"

Nick looked at her. "Marisa, you've got to admit the possibility. Five months ago, she had a miscarriage. Meanwhile, her husband is having an affair."

"Maybe she didn't know."

"How could she not smell the sex on him? Hell, I could." Nick's lip curled with disgust.

Marisa tried to hide the betrayal she felt. Would every man from now on pretend to share her beliefs? "I thought you were on my side. I thought you believed me. And what about Elizabeth Hernandez?"

"We don't know if Elizabeth was murdered. For that matter, we don't know that Carolyn was, either."

"It wasn't suicide." She should never for a moment have doubted Carolyn. She turned away from Nick and went to look out her picture window.

But he appeared beside her and placed a gentle hand on her arm. "You need to be prepared for police speculation, especially with Sheriff Kehr not wanting to investigate Wentworth. The sheriff is going to look for other possibilities."

Marisa's anger resurfaced. "So he's going to trash Carolyn's reputation further?" Was she the only one who wanted people to remember the good things about her friend?

"Probably."

She raised her chin. "Then I'll fight. I have to. I know I'm right." She waited for him to say where he stood.

He nodded. "I'll do what I can."

Marisa let out her breath in relief. "Then I'd better get to the office. I have a wake to plan for tomorrow. Do you want me to drop you back at your cabin?"

"No. I think I'll hang around the sheriff's office today and keep an eye on the investigation."

"I'll drive you there." Marisa hesitated over what she wanted to ask him. Finally, with her cheeks burning, she blurted it out. "Do we smell like sex?"

Nick didn't smile. "Not anymore."

She breathed out and relaxed. "Oh, good. I wasn't sure if my mother would be able to tell."

He cocked his head. "Will it bother you if she knows?"

"A little." Her mother had known she slept with Kevin, but she'd been dating him all her adult life. Nick . . . she'd only known Nick a few days.

He cupped a hand behind her head and drew her to him. Her pulse fluttered madly.

"Only a little?" His voice was husky as his lips descended toward hers.

Marisa nodded, unable to speak. Her lips parted. And then his heat touched her, and with only their lips in contact, she went up in flames. She gripped his biceps as they kissed, leaning into him. Her rioting emotions focused on this man and this moment. He brought sanity to her world.

As he lifted his head, their lips clung, and then the kiss broke. Marisa made a sound of protest.

"Tonight," he said.

*

Marisa dropped Nick at the one-story brick sheriff's office. A small cluster of people gathered around the doors talking, and they turned to stare as she stopped the car. He was aware this was a small town and Marisa was a businesswoman with a reputation to uphold, so he didn't try to kiss her good-bye.

But as she drove away, he wished he had. He'd never had to hide a relationship before, and he found he didn't like it. Sneaking around demeaned what he and Marisa shared together, which, damn it, was more than a sexual liaison. There was a world of difference between Marisa and him and Scott Wentworth and his secretary. Wasn't there?

Nick nodded to the curious citizens and entered the building. He'd been afraid that with the Hernandez death to investigate and the problems with the intake pipe, he'd have to wait several hours to speak with Brian. He'd already decided to help answer the phones and see what he could learn by just being there. But to his surprise, his friend was already at his desk. A quick glance at the sheriff's office showed Sheriff Kehr was still out.

Nick leaned over Brian's desk. "Wentworth's affair with his secretary is a motive for murder."

Brian released a long breath. "I know."

The tension left Nick and he slumped into the side chair. "You know?"

Brian smiled a little. "You can take the boy out of New York City, but you can't take New York City ways out of the boy. I don't think Wentworth was counting on that when he brought Miss Shroyer to town. That 'taking comfort where I can' story didn't fool me for a minute."

"Did you arrest him then?"

Brian shook his head. "Just because he didn't fool me doesn't mean I have enough evidence to arrest him. Brooke Shroyer confirmed his alibi."

Nick ground his teeth in frustration. "You've got to dig deeper into Wentworth's background. There has to be evidence. You can't just let him get away with murder. And what about the Hernandez woman? Did you find evidence at the pond?"

"With last night's storm and the body being submerged all night, there wasn't much of anything. We called in a forensic tech from Montour Falls. He's meeting me here and then we're going to drive back to the Easterling estate together. You were lucky you caught me."

Luck didn't seem so evident from where Nick sat. "What can I do to help?"

Brian smiled. "You want to man the phones again? I know it's a lot to ask while you're on vacation, but we're really stretched thin at the moment."

"If it means you're out finding evidence against Wentworth, I'll do whatever I can." Nick thought of a better idea. "Maybe you could show me how to research Wentworth's background on the computer."

"Sheriff Kehr would have my badge if I did that."

"He wouldn't have to know it was me. You're going to do it anyway as soon as you have time."

"Kehr may be an ass, Nick, but I really like my job here. And I like living in Watkins Glen. If I'm lucky, I'll find a woman like Marisa Avalos and settle down to have a few kids."

Nick bristled, and his stomach lurched. A sharp warning stuck in his throat. He wouldn't be here after this weekend. He had no right to warn Brian away from Marisa. But he couldn't stand the thought of his friend dating her, or, God forbid, sleeping with her. His face warmed with anger. In fact, he couldn't stand the idea of any other man touching Marisa.

"You know," Brian said, "you could settle down with Marisa Avalos and have a few kids. If you'd stay."

"I'm going back to work on Monday, if the shrink clears me. To a job I love. I'm needed there. I make a difference there." He was so used to saying it that he nearly believed it, even if the past six months had proved him wrong.

Brian's gaze was razor sharp. "You could make a difference here, Nick. Look what Marisa is doing to make things happen, to change things."

Yeah, Marisa fought for the truth and for what was right. She championed what was best for the people and the town. She demanded justice and fairness. She was a damn hero and he should know. He'd been one for years. Hell, standing beside her, he'd begun to feel like one again. No wonder he liked her so much.

He plowed a hand through his hair. He couldn't make any decisions until he was cleared to work, and then he'd probably be sucked back into his job. He wouldn't be able to return here soon.

His eye fell on a paper on Brian's desk. Marisa's name jumped out at him. He pointed to it. "What's that?"

Brian picked it up and held it out to Nick. "I had the body shop check all the fluid levels in Marisa's car like you asked me to. You were right. The brake fluid was the only one that was low, and her car had been serviced only a few months ago. She had one of those little reminder stickers in the window."

Nick sat forward and scanned the report. Excitement buzzed inside him like angry bees. "This is it. This is the evidence you need to arrest Wentworth."

But Brian shook his head. "This is a piece of evidence. It shows something happened to the brake fluid in Marisa's car. It doesn't prove who did it."

"Damn it, we know who did it."

"We suspect who did it. We need proof."

"What about fingerprints?"

"It poured last night. Marisa's car is outside at the body shop. Any fingerprints were washed away."

Nick pounded the seat arm. It seemed fate was against them. Or at least someone in Watkins Glen was.

*

It felt odd for Marisa to drive on without Nick because they'd been together for nearly twenty-four hours. As she breezed through her office door, she braced herself to face her mother's questions about her whereabouts during that time.

Her mother looked up from straightening the racks of clothes. "*Mi hija*, is it true about Elizabeth Hernandez?"

All thought of Nick flew from her mind as Marisa sat her mother down and told her everything she knew about Elizabeth.

"In the pond?" Anjelita's eyes filled with tears. "What is happening?"

Marisa clutched her mother's hand. "I don't know, Mamá. Maybe you should come and stay with me for a while."

"Be chased from my home? No." Anjelita shook her head hard.

Marisa chose her words carefully, remembering Nick's warnings about Scott. "But you're so close to the Easterling house."

"You think I am at risk living there? Why? I have lived there since before you were born."

"I don't know. But if you won't come stay with me, will you at least promise to lock your doors from now on?"

"Is it because of Scott Wentworth?" Her mother's brown eyes probed for the truth.

"Mamá, I don't know anything for sure. He's having an affair with his secretary . . . "

"In the Easterling's house? In Carolyn's bed? Oh, the poor child. Wentworth is a despicable man."

"Nick says the sheriff will try to claim Carolyn killed herself because she found out about the affair."

"No." Anjelita's frown was fierce. "It is not true. She would not do that because of a mistress."

Marisa frowned, wondering why her mother was so sure about that. "I want to plan Carolyn's wake for tomorrow. I need to be proactive if I intend to head off the sheriff's claims."

Anjelita lifted her chin. "How can I help?"

Marisa squeezed her mother's hands in appreciation. "I need to find a big enough hall. I need to have her body moved and prepared for viewing. And I need to notify everyone in town."

"Call the funeral home. They can help you arrange the rest. When you have a time set, I will help you call people."

Within an hour, Marisa had made the arrangements and she and her mother spent the rest of the day notifying people about the wake. By six o'clock, Marisa was ready to call it a day.

"Mamá, we've told as many people as we can. Let's go have some dinner."

"I am sorry, *mi hija*, but I have been asked to join the civic society for dinner."

Startled, Marisa looked at her mother. Anjelita's face glowed with happiness and pride. She'd been on the outskirts of the town's society for years, partly due to her heritage, and partly due to working unusual hours as the Easterlings' housekeeper. Now that she was a business owner, Anjelita was part of the heart of the town.

Warmth bloomed in Marisa's chest: pride in her mother, pride in her town. "Have a good time, Mamá. Don't worry about me." When her mother hurried off to her dinner, Marisa realized she was free to be with Nick. With unfettered eagerness, she called him to see where he was.

"I thought maybe you'd changed your mind," he said.

"No. I spent the day notifying the townspeople about Carolyn's wake." She slapped her forehead. She'd completely forgotten him in the rush of events. "Oh, we didn't get to go photographing today. I'm so sorry, Nick."

"It's okay." Relief sounded in his voice. "When I didn't hear from you, I went out on my own."

"Where did you go?" She was disappointed she hadn't got to see the joy in his face when he took pictures.

"Just outside of town. I photographed the fall foliage, what's left of it."

Marisa wanted to be with him badly, but she tried to be polite and think of his needs. "Have you had dinner?"

"Not yet." He was just as polite, just as restrained.

"Would you like to go out to eat?" She hoped he'd say no.

"I'd rather stay in. I stopped at the store in Montour Falls and bought some things for us." His words dripped with sexual innuendo.

Marisa felt all fluttery in her lower belly. "I'm interested. Why don't you meet me at my apartment and we'll have dinner. Then you can show me what you bought."

*

As they showered off any remaining chocolate syrup from their dessert play in bed, Marisa was amazed at how comfortable she felt with Nick. Here he was, a relative stranger, soaping her body as she soaped his and they'd only known each other five days. She'd never showered with Kevin. Of course, she'd never licked chocolate off his cock, either. Kevin was a very traditional man. She realized now that he'd only been going through the motions with her. He'd felt no passion for her. She was amazed the truth didn't hurt anymore.

Marisa didn't have that problem with Nick. She lathered his penis between her hands, rubbing the soap over every inch of him. Nick reached between her legs with a handful of suds. She almost groaned as he cleaned her recently sensitized flesh.

She spread her legs wider and let him soap her thoroughly. She did the same to his testicles and anus.

They stared into each other's eyes as they slid slick hands over one another, teasing, tantalizing, re-awakening desire. His eyes were melted chocolate, his skin flushed with arousal. They were both breathing hard.

When Nick turned her, Marisa thought he would take her then. But he pushed her under the water, sliding his hands over her flesh to help clear the soap. He brushed his palms over her nipples, back and forth, until she was sure they were clean. He quickly rinsed himself, turned off the water and pulled Marisa from the shower.

They dried each other in a hurry. Nick had another hard-on, so Marisa knew they were heading back for the bed and another bout of lovemaking.

Nick dragged the chocolate-coated sheet of Visqueen from

the bed and piled it in a corner. But instead of reaching for her, he reached inside the drug store bag. Pulling out a little box, he removed two items. One was a condom.

"Do you want to do the honors?" He offered it to her.

Marisa wanted to know what the other item was, but she took the condom and smoothed it on him, caressing him as she did so.

As soon as he was sheathed, Nick carried her down to the bed and covered her mouth with his. She was hungry for the taste of him without chocolate, the taste that was singularly him. His mouth was hot and demanding. He kissed her again and again until she felt lightheaded. Her legs tangled with his, his hot erection pressed tightly against her lower belly.

She couldn't get enough of kissing him, but one of his hands reached between them to caress her nipple. She gasped. Nick had spent a long time sucking the chocolate off her nipples and they were still tender. Her open mouth allowed his tongue to penetrate. He touched her tongue, caressing it as he caressed her breast. She stroked him too, his tongue, his back, and his tight round buttocks. His body was a work of art with every lean muscle delineated.

Nick freed a second hand to caress both her breasts. Marisa rubbed her lower lips against his condom-coated cock. Her body was slick against the latex. As much as she liked the preliminaries, Nick hadn't entered her body during their last bout of lovemaking, and she ached to be filled with him.

"Nick, please, I need you inside me."

"Don't you like this?" He pulled on her nipples and she groaned.

"I like everything you do to me, but I like it best when you're inside me."

"You've got to be ready for me."

"I am."

"I'm going to take a long time."

"How long?" A thrill ran through her vagina.

"A *long* time."

"Do it."

He reached around her to the nightstand for the other packet. "What is it?"

"You'll see."

Then Nick kissed her so she couldn't see, but she felt him adjust his cock, and then he shoved inside her.

It felt good, he felt right. Marisa adjusted her body to accept him fully.

"How's that feel." He sounded happy.

"Good. Really good."

"Do you want better?"

She pictured herself with her legs up on his shoulders and him driving hard. "Yes."

He reached between them, and then he thrust deeply into her. Something between them vibrated across her clitoris. Marisa jerked and shrieked her pleasure.

But Nick gathered her close to him as he made love, pressing into her clitoris and holding her to him. His thrusts and the vibration made her tighten inside. The pleasure wound around her lower body, drawing ever tighter, until orgasm arced through her. Marisa bucked against Nick. He pressed the vibrator tight to her widely spread legs.

Suddenly a second orgasm swept her away. She gasped and clung to him, milking his pistoning cock.

But Nick didn't come. He did pull out of her and rolled her over on her stomach. Then he raised her buttocks and thrust home. Marisa groaned. The vibrator touched a sensitive spot between her vagina and anus. It was too much stimulation. She tried to wriggle away, but Nick's strong hands held her hips firmly in place.

She cried out over and over, until finally orgasm consumed her again. Her entire lower body tingled. She lifted her hips to receive Nick inside again and again.

He was breathing hard as he pulled out of her. She couldn't

help her protest. But he climbed off the bed, pulled her back to him, and thrust inside of her once more. Marisa groaned deeply.

Nick pulled her hard against his pubic bone over and over, filling every part of her as deeply as he could. She convulsed again, deep inside.

Then he rolled her to her back and plunged deep. The vibrator hit her clitoris once more and she screamed as orgasm overtook her. As sated as she felt, she was glad when Nick raised her heels to his shoulders. He crouched over her, plunging fiercely inside. Helpless, Marisa rode yet another orgasm. Her body felt aflame with pleasure.

Their lovemaking seemed to go on and on. Her body took everything Nick offered, every deep and penetrating thrust. Her body was Nick's plaything to make dance with orgasm.

Suddenly the vibration stopped.

Nick dragged in a breath. "Oh well. It was fun while it lasted."

Three urgent thrusts later, he came with violent intensity. Collapsing onto her, he lay gasping. Marisa's legs slid to the bed.

She'd never made love like that before. When she caught her breath, she asked, "What was that?"

"Stimulator ring." She felt him smile against her cheek. "Even men like vibrators, you know."

She hadn't known. In fact, she hadn't even considered how it felt to him. "So it feels good to you?"

He rose up on his elbow and smiled at her. Her stomach flipped over. "Damn good. Especially when I'm inside you."

She licked her lips and noted, "It really increases your stamina."

"It's hard to come with that damn ring squeezing me."

Marisa smiled. "How many of those did you buy?"

He pursed his lips in a mock pout. "What, that wasn't a good enough performance for you?"

She laughed and reassured him. "I loved it."

His face smoothed into seriousness. "I bought four of them. The vibrator lasts twenty minutes."

My God, they'd made love for twenty minutes? "Come here." She opened her arms and he eased down into them. Their lips met, clung.

She never wanted this time with Nick to end.

CHAPTER 15

"Marisa! Fire!"

Nick's shout tore Marisa from sleep. Smoke clogged her throat and made her cough. She felt lethargic with tiredness. Then Nick dragged her from the bed and onto her feet where she stood shivering.

"Get dressed. We've got to get out of here." He left her side and she heard rustling as he searched for his clothes.

Her brain felt mushy. Where had she left her clothes and why didn't Nick turn on the lights? She turned toward the nightstand, but the numbers on her electric clock weren't visible. How strange.

"Marisa, move!" Nick filled her arms with clothes.

She struggled with her bra for a moment, and then gave up. She tugged on her shirt and shorts. Before she could slip on her sneakers, Nick grabbed her hand and pulled her out of the bedroom into the hall. The smoke seemed thicker here.

"Stay low."

Coughing bent her over anyway. She couldn't get a lungful of clean air.

"Lower." Nick pushed her into a crouch. He kept his hands against her sides, guiding her through a doorway.

Furniture loomed out of the darkness, startling her. She hadn't thought her apartment was this big, but it seemed to take forever to reach the living room. There a bright light bathed the scene in the reddish colors of hell. Flames licked at her drapes.

Nick spat a blistering curse.

"The house is on fire!" How had Marisa not connected smoke with the possibility her home would be consumed. "My things!"

"Forget them." Nick reached the door and placed his palm on it. He hissed and snatched it away. "Is there another way out?"

Marisa choked on the smoke and her fear as she watched the voracious flames crawling up her walls.

"Marisa!"

She tore her gaze from the tongues of flame. "There's a back staircase through the kitchen."

He shoved her in that direction. "Show me."

They made their way through the dining room. As they entered the kitchen, a loud whoosh behind them jerked Marisa's head around. Flame ran up her dining room wall. She shrieked, drawing in a lungful of smoke.

As she coughed, Nick dragged her through the kitchen. He yanked on the doorknob, but the door wouldn't come open.

"It's locked," Marisa said.

"Then unlock it."

"I need the key." Where did she keep it? It seemed so hard to think.

"We don't have time for this." Nick took a step back and lashed his foot at the door. The boom sounded loud in the room. He kicked the door again.

The door might be a hundred years old, but it was of sturdy construction. It would take too long to break it down. Then Marisa remembered where she kept the key. She darted away from Nick.

"Marisa, come back here!"

But the roaring sounds coming from the other rooms terrified her. They needed to get out fast. She felt for the key in the wall pot and thrust herself between Nick and the door. Inserting the key, she wrenched the door open. Nick pushed her down into the stygian depths of the stairwell.

"Keep a hand on the wall," he said.

They met someone on the landing. "The house is on fire!" Dinah Briner's voice quavered. She had a second floor apartment too.

Nick prodded them. "Down the stairs."

The outer door opened onto cool, clean night air that slapped Marisa in the face. Another figure stumbled out of the door behind them, gasping. Jeremy Scrynecki—who had the third-floor apartment—fell to his knees, coughing hard.

"Jeremy!" Dinah rushed to his assistance.

"Who else lives here?" Nick asked.

Now that she could breathe, she could think, too. "Mr. and Mrs. Loboschefski have the first floor apartment on the right. They're elderly. Arlene Jarzabek has the other, but she works nights."

"Stay here, all of you, but move back from the house," Nick said. "I'll see if the others got out."

Dinah had gotten Jeremy to his feet. Now she tugged the younger man away from the house.

Marisa was thankful Arlene was at work. Then she remembered Arlene's toy poodle, inherited when her mother died last year. Peaches was her pride and joy. The poor little dog!

A whoosh made them all gasp and look upwards. Flames licked the outside of the second floor. Dinah sobbed and Jeremy patted the older woman with an awkward attempt at sympathy.

Marisa looked at Arlene's apartment where flames danced in one window. Her stomach twisted as she pictured the poor, terrified animal.

Sprinting for the front of the house, Marisa ignored the others' cries to stay back. Nick was busy with the elderly Loboschefskis. He didn't have time for little Peaches.

The front door hung askew. Smoke choked the hall and boiled out onto the porch. She thought she heard Peaches' terrified barking. Arlene's door was unlocked. Her living room was engulfed in flames. In the dining room, poor Peaches cowered near the window, barking frantically, her fur bathed in scarlet light. Her barks were terrified and they tore at Marisa's heart.

She coughed hard trying to draw a lungful of air. "Peaches, come here!"

The little dog whined in terror.

"Peaches, come!"

The poodle paced, looking wild.

Marisa would have to cross the flames to her. There was no way the old, arthritic dog could jump over the sill if Marisa broke the window from the outside.

Marisa bent as low as possible and dragged in as much air as she could. She studied the flames. There was just enough room to get to the dog if she ran a zigzag path.

Suddenly Peaches yelped. A piece of the ceiling had dropped, curling up into ashes as Marisa watched.

It was run now or condemn Peaches to a horrible death. Marisa rose to a crouch and ran the gauntlet of fire. Her lungs burned. Her eyes stung. Pain seared across her forearm.

She got within an arm's length of Peaches and reached out and grabbed whatever fur she could. Peaches yelped, but Marisa swung the little dog up into her arms, turning as she did.

Thick smoke boiled between her and the door. Her heart seized with fear. But Peaches wriggled and Marisa gathered her courage and ran. Flames reached for her, singed her. Marisa leaped the last few feet. Strong arms jerked her out of the burning apartment and pushed her toward fresh air.

As she bent over in the yard, coughing, hands beat hard on her back.

"Stop it," she said.

"You're on fire." Nick sounded angry.

Peaches whined and she loosened her painful grip on the dog. The poodle began to shiver.

"What the hell did you go in there for? You said the woman was at work. Are you crazy?"

As the sound of sirens split the night, Marisa straightened to face him. Nick's wild eyes reflected the orange flames.

"I'm the professional, Marisa. It's my job to rescue people."

"What about dogs?"

His gaze dropped to Peaches and widened. The dog's shaking had finally lessened. Her fur reeked of smoke. It was a miracle she hadn't been overcome by it.

"I didn't think you had time for Peaches."

"You risked your life for a dog?"

"Peaches is all Arlene has left of her mother. I couldn't let her burn to death. Did you get the Loboschefskis out?"

He didn't answer for a moment. "Yes. Mr. Loboschefski will need to go to the hospital to be checked out."

The town's fire engine pulled up in front of the house, followed closely by the paramedics and two sheriff's cars.

Nick gripped her forearm and Marisa gasped. He jerked his hand away and studied her injury. "That burn's going to need treatment." Anger laced his words.

He wrapped his arm around her waist instead and pulled her out of the way. They joined the other tenants huddled in a group. The white-haired Mr. Loboschefski sat on the ground with a blanket around him.

"Everything I own is in there." Dinah was in her forties and recently divorced.

"My sketches." Jeremy's voice caught.

"My photos of Carolyn," Marisa said.

"I was going to use them for the wake." To her surprise, a tear slid down her cheek.

"You saved Peaches." Mr. Loboschefski surrendered to a coughing fit.

The paramedics approached them. "Is anyone hurt?"

Nick gave them a rundown of everyone's injuries. The medics got Mr. Loboschefski on oxygen. When Mrs. Loboschefski collapsed into the grass, they immediately went to work on her.

Marisa handed Peaches to Dinah. The little dog whimpered in distress, but Marisa's arm and shoulder had begun to burn and her body to shake. Nick wrapped his arms around her, but even his fierce heat couldn't warm her. They could have died if they hadn't woken.

She heard Brian Nash's voice. "What happened, Nick?"

"It can't be an accident this time." Nick's voice was fierce but low, his grip around her tight. "The odds of this fire being natural would be astronomical. If I hadn't been here . . . "

"I'll tell the fire chief to look for signs of arson."

Marisa shook harder. Arson meant attempted murder.

"Wentworth had better have an airtight alibi," Nick said. "Or I want him in jail."

"I'll interview him myself."

"I don't like it that bad things are happening in this town. I want Marisa to be safe."

She turned in Nick's arms in time to see Sheriff Kehr push his way into their group. "Did I hear you accuse Scott Wentworth of this? He wouldn't burn down an apartment building."

Marisa was tired of the buffoon, but Nick spoke first. "You don't know what he'd do, Sheriff. You don't know anything about Wentworth since you've never investigated him. And if you block any investigation into his whereabouts, I'll call the FBI to begin an investigation into your obstruction of justice. You're a lawman, not Wentworth's lackey. A woman's life is in danger. Do your job and find out who wants her out of the way."

The sheriff's face turned brick red, but he signaled Brian away and the two talked urgently where Marisa couldn't hear. She watched the firemen fight the fire, but the 100-year-old wood was no match for the flames. Tears misted her eyes. She hadn't lived here long, but it had been her first home since she became an adult. She'd loved the smoking porch and the spaciousness of her rooms, the old-fashioned graciousness of the Victorian.

Now she'd have to start over from scratch. Another part of her life was over. Her teeth chattered.

Nick glanced at the paramedics who were busy working on the Loboschefskis. "I'm taking you to the hospital."

"I don't need a hospital." Her voice shook like her body.

"Yeah, you do. That burn needs treatment."

She'd forgotten about the burn. The mention of it woke the heat in her skin.

"C'mon." Nick turned her toward the apartment's parking lot.

"I don't have my purse." Marisa had no identification and no insurance card, no money or credit cards. Or anything else she owned. And the only clothes she had were the ones she was wearing.

"I managed to grab your purse as we went through the house. It's in the grass by the back door."

"Oh." He'd been thinking about her needs even then. How like him.

Nick snatched up her purse and towed her toward his car, which was parked away from the house.

"What about my rental car?" She didn't want to be responsible for that.

"I'll ask one of your neighbors to move it. Go ahead and get in the car."

She handed him the keys and climbed in. He was back in a jiffy and maneuvered his car around the emergency vehicles out front and turned onto the street. Marisa saw they were loading Mr. Loboschefski into the ambulance.

She looked back as they drove away. Flames licked at the dark sky. Grief choked her. Could she survive losing anything else this week?

*

Nick paced the hospital corridor while the medical staff treated Marisa's burns. He'd tried to sit down, but his nervous energy needed an outlet. He could have lost Marisa today.

He jerked in the other direction and paced back. That stupid, brave, caring woman had risked her life to save a dog. His fists clenched. He probably would have done the same if she'd asked him to, but she hadn't. She'd faced the gauntlet of fire alone. He was supposed to be the hero. It was his job to risk life and limb, not hers.

His chest felt tight. He didn't want to think about the repercussions if she'd died in that burning apartment.

He wanted to smash Wentworth's face. No one else could be responsible. As he pivoted in the other direction, he nearly careened into Marisa's doctor. The doctor held out his hands to stop the collision.

"I'm giving her IV antibiotics and I want her to stay here for a few hours to make sure she doesn't go into shock, but she should be fine," Dr. Consear said. "There was one small third-degree burn. The rest were only second degree. Eventually she can have plastic surgery to remove the scar."

Some of Nick's tension bled away. "Thanks, doctor."

"I put her on oxygen just while she's here because she breathed in a lot of smoke. She's very lucky." He patted Nick on the shoulder and headed for the nurses' station.

Nick braced himself to face Marisa. As he entered the small exam room, he saw her arm was tucked into one half of her hospital gown. The staff had covered her breast on the exposed side, the side where white bandages spotted her forearm and bicep. He knew there was another bandage on her shoulder blade where falling debris had burned her. His stomach tightened at the thought. He bent down and kissed her. She reeked of smoke. So did he.

"The doctor says I have to stay for a few hours, but the burns aren't as bad as you thought." He thought Marisa was trying to be positive.

He took hold of her hand, smoothing his thumb over her knuckles. "He told me. But they could have been worse, much worse. Don't you know how dangerous it is to enter a burning building?"

"You went in after the Loboschefskis."

"I work for the fire department."

"As an EMT."

Nick flinched. The reminder hit him on the raw. "You could have been killed. People die in fires, even firefighters."

She glared at him, but then she frowned. "Someone you knew died in a fire?"

It shouldn't surprise him that she'd figure it out; after all, she seemed to understand him. He nodded. "My dad was a fireman. He was killed in a three alarm two years ago."

Now she caressed his hand with both of hers. "Did you work with him?"

"No. The department doesn't want family members to work together. My brother also works for the NYFD, but he works out of a station in Queens."

"Is he a fireman or an EMT like you?"

"A fireman. I come from a long line of firefighters. I'm the black sheep. My dad couldn't understand that I wanted to work the medical end of the fire department. He always thought he'd gone wrong with me somehow."

Marisa squeezed his hand. "He didn't go wrong. Tell me how he died."

Somehow, the words came out. He'd told the department shrink, but he hadn't spoken about it to anyone else. "It was a bad blaze, an old structure that burned like a supernova. The floor above him caved in, and he and his partner were crushed under the burning debris. The rest of his station couldn't get to them because of the flames. I was treating the injured, so I couldn't leave them."

Her eyes were sympathetic. "You were there when he died?"

Nick nodded. "My station got called out last. His was first on the scene. I heard what happened over the radio. I wanted to help find him. I knew I could save him if they'd just let me go in. But in New York City the EMTs don't help fight the fires."

The scene replayed in his mind for the millionth time—his captain holding him back, two firefighters bringing in a third on a stretcher, the man screaming with the pain of his burns. Nick's duty was to the injured man, his captain had reminded him.

"I'm sorry about your dad. You save a lot of people as an EMT."

Some of what he'd been feeling these past months escaped his tight hold and found its way into words. "Not nearly as many as I used to.

It seems like there have been a lot of suicides the past six months, a lot of senseless violence. I've had to pronounce a lot of people lately. I try and I try, but I just can't seem to make a difference."

"Nick, the kind of job you have in a place like New York City, you're bound to see more bad things than other people. It's not because you don't make a difference. You do."

He couldn't accept what she said as the truth. Not anymore. "Maybe I should have been a fireman like my dad wanted. I didn't have any problem going in after the Loboschefskis. I'd be able to save more people that way."

She threaded her fingers with his, as though she could hold him back from running right out to become a fireman. "We're both pretty rocky right now. It's not the time to make life-altering decisions."

The door opened behind him. Nick turned to see the DNA doctor, Ziad Smail, with a wide smile on his face.

"When they told me you were here, Miss Avalos, I couldn't believe it. I have good news. You're Andrew Easterling's daughter."

CHAPTER 16

"Andrew Easterling was my father?" In a week where Marisa's known world had crumbled like buildings in a strong earthquake, it rocked once more. This conversation was déjà vu like the one she'd had with her fiancé days ago and she was just as disbelieving now as then. "Are you certain?"

Dr. Smail's smile was blinding in contrast to his swarthy complexion. "Let's just say that enough alleles matched with Carolyn Wentworth to make it a ninety-six percent certainty that she was your blood relative." He bounced on the heels of his feet.

Marisa swallowed the emotion clogging her throat. Carolyn had been her sister. She managed a polite, "Thank you, Dr. Smail."

"I'll call Watkins Glen immediately and let them know."

"Wait!" She swallowed again. "I need to talk to my mother first. I'll call Mr. Jantzen as soon as I'm done."

He nodded. "I understand. You're in shock right now. Congratulations!" He left, beaming.

No sooner had the door shut, than the dam holding back Marisa's emotions burst. She covered her face and wept. This was one loss too many, this loss of truth and of self.

Nick sat on the gurney and gathered her to him. She didn't want to burden him more than she already had, so she tried to push him away.

"You can cry on me."

Still she balked, wanting, yet not wanting comfort. "My mother lied to me, for twenty-six years. My father lived right next door. He was at my house nearly every day. He played with me, he taught me things, and he helped me choose a college. And all that time, they kept their secret!" Bitterness was a sour taste in her mouth.

"Maybe he didn't know."

She stared at him, her eyes widening in horror. "You think my mother slept with so many men she didn't know who my father was?" It was worse than thinking her mother had lied. Had her mother been the town tramp all those years ago? Scott's scathing remarks echoed in her head.

A sob worked its way out of Marisa's throat, then another. "Oh my God. I was better off not knowing."

Nick hugged her tighter. "I meant maybe she never told him."

Which meant her mother was either a slut or a liar. Another part of the foundation of her life crumbled. All these years she thought she'd been a by-product of love. Instead, she might have been a one-night-stand. She felt her heart breaking.

As Marisa wept, Nick held her and rubbed her unburned shoulder. "Carolyn was my sister. All those years I felt as close as one, and all that time I was. They took that from us." She cried harder.

"Would you have loved her more if you'd known?" Nick asked in a low voice against her temple.

"Yes. No, I guess not. But I would have kept in better touch with her." Carolyn wouldn't have had to keep her miscarriage to herself. Guilt burned in Marisa's gut.

"My brother and I have barely spoken since my dad died." Nick's voice sounded strained. "I think he blames me for not saving my dad, but I don't know for sure. I can't bring myself to ask him. So you see, blood doesn't make a difference."

The pain in Nick's statement stopped her tears. He'd known his father all his life, yet his father hadn't been able to accept his choices. Marisa didn't know if Andrew Easterling had known she was his daughter, but he had accepted her without reservation. He'd been a loving father to her in so many ways. He'd treated her exactly as he'd treated Carolyn.

"I need to talk to my mother." Marisa wiped her face and reached to pull out the IV, but Nick stopped her.

"I won't let you risk your life just so you can talk about something that happened twenty-six years ago. It's waited this long. It can wait a little longer."

Her rage found an outlet. "What right have you got to tell me what to do?"

"I'm the man who would have died trying to save you if you hadn't made it out of that apartment."

Her breath caught, amazed by his words and the intensity with which he spoke them, but then she realized what he'd meant. Nick was a rescuer. He saved people, or tried to. He'd worked himself into burnout trying to save people after his father died. He'd been playing her hero since they met. It was in his DNA.

But the blunt businessman was in her DNA. She knew now why she was good with numbers—because her father had been. "I don't need to be rescued, Nick. All I need is the truth. And I need it before I face the townspeople standing next to my sister's casket."

He sighed. "All right. I'll drive you home."

*

They picked up Marisa's mother at her shop and Nick drove them in silence to the little cottage on the Easterling estate. There was a potential it might be hers now. The lawyers would have to fight over that, but that fight was for later.

Nick gave her a lingering look, but didn't try to kiss her in front of her mother, for which Marisa was grateful. He turned and walked down the driveway as she and her mother entered the little cottage.

Anjelita hadn't said anything from the moment she'd looked at Marisa's face in the shop. Now she pressed, "Are you really all right, *mi hija*?" Marisa had called her from the hospital when they arrived at the ER.

"Yes, Mamá. I'll have a scar, but no other injuries." The pleasantries took more effort than they should.

"You could have been killed." Despite what her mother might sense in Marisa, she worried over her child's health before anything else.

"I know. Mamá, please sit down." Marisa couldn't wait any longer for the truth.

Anjelita studied her face, and then seemed to wilt into her favorite chair.

"I got the DNA test results while I was at the hospital. Andrew Easterling was my father."

Anjelita nodded. "And now you know."

"Did you know, Mamá?" Marisa spoke as her mother's child, but what she asked wasn't childish.

Anjelita's head snapped up. "Of course I knew."

"You said you'd had many lovers."

"I know how to prevent a child, Marisa, and other things. I may have been a poor Catholic, but I was not stupid."

"Then how did it happen?" Marisa needed to know.

"The condom broke. It was during the weekend Andrew and I spent together." Anjelita hesitated and then added. "Before I knew he had a wife."

Marisa did the math in her head. There was barely nine months difference between Carolyn and her. She guessed, "Carolyn had just been born and Mrs. Easterling paralyzed."

"I did not know that then."

"He spent the weekend with you while his newborn child was in the hospital and his wife was on life support?" Oh, it just got worse and worse. She sank into a chair.

"Andrew went a little crazy thinking they were both going to die. He told me this later. All I knew then was that I had found the man I wanted to marry and I gave myself to the man I thought would be my husband."

Marisa's fists clenched on her knees. "He was already married."

"I found that out later, but it was too late. You were already conceived and I was hopelessly in love."

Marisa had to swallow the lump in her throat before she could speak. "He's the man you never got over?"

"Yes."

"Then why did you become his housekeeper?"

"I have always done the best I could for you."

Marisa wondered about the change in subject. "Yes, you have."

"Everything I did, I did for you."

"I know."

"I told Andrew about you. His wife could not have more children so he wanted to adopt you. You would have been Carolyn's sister in name. But I would not let him have you."

"He just wanted you to give me away?"

"He wanted Carolyn to have a sibling. He hoped for a son. When I would not give you up, he asked me to live there, to let you be raised with Carolyn. How could I refuse? He gave us a house. He'd be able to see you every day and be a father to you."

"So that one weekend tied you to him forever."

"No, *mi hija*." Sadness filled Anjelita's eyes.

Marisa braced for worse.

"We were bound, Andrew and I, from the moment we met. He moved me into his house and his life . . . "

"No." The rumors couldn't be true. Marisa wanted to clap her hands over her ears and block out the truth.

"We loved each other very much, your father and I."

"No, no, no. Mamá, you had an affair with my father?"

"Not an affair, no. But I was his lover until the day he died. He was faithful to me."

"And unfaithful to his wife." Marisa could not contain her bitterness. She rocketed from the chair and paced to the window. It was sunny outside. It should be stormy, like she felt inside.

"Not unfaithful," her mother said. "She could not be his wife in that way. But I could. She agreed this arrangement worked for everyone."

Marisa spun around, incredulous. "She knew? You talked about it with her?"

"I was not a prostitute, *mi hija*." Anjelita's tone was sharp. "I was his other wife, in all but name. I did what his first wife could not do. But without her approval, I would not have kept his house, raised his children, or been his lover."

The world had gone insane. Marisa could no longer make sense of it. "You could have married someone else, had other children."

"No. There was no one but Andrew for me. He wanted to marry me. He bought the rings and everything. He wanted legal standing for our relationship and for you. Andrew said men had had more than one wife in the Bible. He hated that we couldn't live openly as a couple. It was hard for me not to be able to spend the whole night in his arms. Slipping from his bed in the night made what we shared seem sordid. Committed love is anything but sordid.

"We discussed driving to another city where no one knew us and getting married. But I didn't want shame to come to his wife if anyone found out he was a bigamist. Such an ugly word. I compromised, because he wanted it so badly."

Marisa tensed. "Compromised? How?"

"We spoke our wedding vows to each other in private. In the garden. We renewed them every five years. Andrew was just as eager that last time as he'd been the first time."

"But it wasn't legal. You weren't really married."

"In our hearts and minds we were. What I shared with your father wasn't an affair, Marisa. Not for either of us. We sealed our lives together. Till death do us part."

Marisa couldn't begin to understand her parents' relationship. Her legs felt rubbery, so she returned to her chair to try to understand the rest. "Why didn't you tell me he was my father?"

"It is hard for a child to keep a secret. During your early years, we kept our love for each other hidden. Later, when it would have been all right to tell you, there was Carolyn to consider. Andrew did not want to hurt her."

"Why didn't you tell me the truth after . . . my father . . . died?"

"I had loved him for twenty-seven years, *mi hija*. My man was dead. I wanted to die too. I had no job, no lover, no life. I am sorry I did not think of telling you until Carolyn died."

Marisa sat wordless. Her mother had grieved silently for her father. All those lost looks hadn't been a woman wondering how she'd pay her bills, but how she'd go on without the man she loved. Since she'd met Nick, Marisa began to understand a little of how her mother must feel.

"Daddy really loved you, Mamá?" Marisa swallowed and winced. "It wasn't just the sex?"

Anjelita's smile was strained. "He told me so every day, even when we were not in bed."

Marisa tried not to think that her forty-six-year-old mother had been sexually active until a year ago. With her father. Andrew Easterling.

"I will never love again. I am one of those women who can only love one man. That is why I held onto Andrew in the only way I could." Her eyes filled with tears.

Marisa went to her mother, kneeling by her chair. She took hold of her mother's hands. "Tell me about my father, Mamá."

Her mother smiled a watery smile and began.

*

"How could Wentworth have an alibi?" Nick asked Brian. He'd walked to the smoking remains of Marisa's apartment house and found her car parked in the street with the keys inside. Then he'd driven to the sheriff's office. After seeing the charred remains of Marisa's home and being reminded how close they'd come to dying, he was in no mood to hear bad news.

"He was with his secretary . . . "

"Again?"

"You should talk," Brian said with some asperity.

"Marisa's the intended victim. Leave our relationship out of this."

"You know I was joking when I said to guard her."

Nick ground his teeth together. "Somebody has to protect her, but that's not why I'm with her."

"I know that." Brian checked his tone. "Listen, I even felt the hood of Wentworth's car. It was cold."

"His mistress has a car too, you know. Besides, Marisa walks home from her mother's house all the time. It's not far."

"What about the alibi?"

"He's sleeping with her. Of course she's going to lie for him." Nick raked his hands through his hair.

Brian pierced him with a look. "Would you lie for Marisa?"

Nick opened his mouth to deny he'd lie for anyone. Instead, what came out was, "I'd die for her." He began to shake.

"Man, I can't believe it." Brian shook his head. "I hope it doesn't come to that."

"Then you'd better break Wentworth's alibi. Get his mistress in here and grill her." Nick lowered his voice so only Brian could hear. "Marisa got the DNA test results at the hospital this morning. She's Easterling's daughter."

"Jesus." Brian ran a hand down his face, staring at Nick. "What are you saying?"

"I think Wentworth knows. I don't know if Easterling knew, but I suspect he did. Maybe there was something in his house that tipped Wentworth off."

"If there was, then why didn't Easterling split the inheritance in his will?"

Nick threw up his hands. "Who knows? I'm sure the man didn't expect to die that young."

"I guess not. Who does?" Brian walked around his desk and sat down, signaling Nick to do the same. "How'd Marisa take it?"

Nick settled in the other chair. "How do you think? She cried. This has been a very emotional week for her."

"And on top of everything else, she's sleeping with you."

"Yeah." Nick wished he could give her up in his last two days in town, but he couldn't. He needed her.

Thinking aloud, he said, "If Wentworth killed his wife to get her money . . . "

"That's not proven."

"Then he wouldn't want Marisa in the way, either. Did the fire department find evidence at the scene?"

Brian shook his head and picked up a small tablet. His gaze moved over the words written on it.

"It looked like the first floor tenant left her stove on when she went to work. The fire spread from her apartment into Marisa's above it."

"Does the tenant confirm leaving the stove on?"

"She doesn't remember. She was hysterical until she found out her dog was safe at the vet's."

Nick felt a twinge of guilt for yelling at Marisa over the dog. "Can we prove she didn't leave the stove on?"

"Most of the house burned, Nick. It's a total loss. The fire department did confirm there was no accelerant used."

"He wanted it to look like an accident. Can you call in a forensic specialist from New York City or the FBI?"

"And tell them what? That we don't believe the accidents are really accidents? I don't think a specialist will come here on that basis."

Nick pounded one fist into the other. "Damn it, Brian, do you want to see Marisa killed?"

"No. God, no."

"Then do something about Wentworth."

CHAPTER 17

Marisa stood beside Carolyn's open casket and greeted mourners. The mortuary had done a magnificent job hiding the damage done by the train. Still, Marisa couldn't bear to look, because she knew what the strategically placed flowers covered.

She still couldn't believe Carolyn was her sister, but most of the town could. She'd notified the lawyer and the mayor, and it seemed they'd told everyone else.

"I'm sorry for your loss," one of her high school classmates said to her now. "I had biology class with your sister."

Marisa nodded, unable to speak for a moment. The silent refrain *if only I'd known* beat in her mind.

"So how does it feel knowing you're Andrew Easterling's illegitimate daughter?" The woman's blue eyes sparkled with ill-concealed curiosity and speculation.

"I'm still in shock." What else could Marisa say?

"Yeah, I guess you would be. But you practically lived with him all your life, so you kind of knew your dad."

"Yes." How many times today would thoughtless statements like that hurt her, reminding her that she'd lived a lie?

The classmate shook Marisa's hand and moved on. Marisa had stood by the casket for an hour as townspeople filed through to pay their respects. It didn't look like the influx would lessen any time soon.

Anjelita moved among the tables at the back of the town hall refilling refreshments. Marisa felt separated from her mother for the first time ever. Marisa was blood relation to Carolyn, but Anjelita wasn't. Even though her mother had helped raise Carolyn, blood was what really mattered today.

Marisa wondered if her mother took the servant role now for

the same reason she'd taken it twenty-six years ago—to hide her real role. In this case, that of surrogate mother.

How had her mother hidden her passionate love for Andrew Easterling all those years? Marisa and Carolyn were curious, intelligent girls. How had they missed Andrew and Anjelita carrying on an affair right under their noses?

As townspeople shared anecdotes about Carolyn, Marisa sorted through her own memories of her parents. They had stayed in close proximity when in the same room. They seemed to work as a pair on any task. As she thought hard about it, there was almost always time when her parents were together that they went missing. Five minutes here, ten there, an hour. So that's how they'd hidden their affair, in plain sight.

"Marisa."

Her reverie burst at her ex-fiancé's familiar voice. "Hi, Kevin. I didn't expect to see you here." She winced at her words. "Sorry. I didn't mean it like that."

"I know what you meant. I knew Carolyn for years through you, remember? She was a good friend to you."

Marisa couldn't help asking, "Do you think I was a good friend to her?"

"Of course you were. You treat everyone well. That's why you're such an important part of this town. I'm sorry about Carolyn." He hugged her.

Her body didn't come alive like it did when she came into contact with Nick's. Kevin didn't set her body aflame like Nick did.

Kevin released her. "I'm leaving tonight. I came by to say good-bye."

She clutched his arm, even now afraid to lose this part of her past. "Already?"

"Dr. Handler knows I'm anxious to fly to California, so he released me. He says he's glad to work full-time for a while. So I'll be surfing by the weekend. He says to tell you Peaches is fine."

Unexpectedly, Marisa's eyes misted. "I'm glad you stopped by."

"I'm really sorry it didn't work between us. I heard you've been seeing a friend of Deputy Nash's. I hope that works out better for you."

Marisa couldn't respond through her tight throat. Nick would be home by the weekend, too.

Kevin leaned down to kiss her and she let him because they had a history together, although part of it had been make-believe. When he walked away, she dabbed her eyes. Her life had been a house of cards that had come crashing down.

*

Nick watched Marisa's ex-fiancé kiss her, then watched her wipe away her tears. His fists clenched at his sides. In his head, he'd known she hadn't gotten over Kevin yet. Too bad his heart had hoped differently.

She was a loyal woman. She'd stayed with her fiancé all through college and vet school. It was one of the qualities Nick admired in her. But he hated that that loyalty meant she wasn't ready for more with him. He should break it off with her before they got hurt worse than they would.

"That one did not set my Marisa aflame," Anjelita whispered from beside him.

"What one?"

"Kevin." Anjelita nodded at the blonde man talking to people as he made his way to the door.

Nick wasn't about to tell Marisa's mother he was sleeping with her. "Flame burns. Marisa learned that this morning."

"Where you were with her, in her apartment, in her bed."

Whoops. "Anjelita . . . ."

"You make her burn. I see it when she looks at you, and you at her."

He was uncomfortable talking about what amounted to an affair, although this woman had carried on a twenty-six-year affair with Marisa's father. Who better to understand? "I care for her a great deal."

"Yet you will hurt her."

"Yes. I don't want to, but I have to go back to work." He'd thought there'd never be anything as compelling as his job. But then he'd met Marisa.

"Your work gives your life meaning."

He nodded. "Yes, very much."

"Marisa told me how much your work hurt you."

It surprised him that Marisa had discussed him in depth with her mother. "Not hurt exactly."

Anjelita nodded. "You are a hero. You need to save people."

"Yes." He'd always thought of himself as a hero, but he seemed so flawed lately.

"My Marisa is a hero too."

He looked at the topic of their discussion, so beautiful in a sheer over satin navy pantsuit someone had loaned her. "She is indeed."

"Perhaps you need a hero."

Confused, Nick turned to Marisa's mother, but she had already stepped away. What had she meant?

They took a short supper break, where Nick saw to it that Marisa ate a sandwich. She gave him a weak smile. He wished they were alone so he could take her in his arms and comfort her, but this was stolen time. He could hear the mourners in the hall waiting for her to return.

The hours dragged on. At the time the wake was scheduled to end, mourners were still lined up to the door. The local mortuary told Marisa they would delay until everyone had paid their respects.

Around eight o'clock, the last of the mourners hugged Marisa. As the woman walked away, Marisa drooped. As though that was the signal, the morticians came to close the casket, murmuring low words to Marisa as they handled her sister's body.

Nick moved forward and took Marisa's hand. "Let's go home." The need to take care of her overwhelmed him.

She nodded. "I'm glad everyone had a chance to say good-bye.

Carolyn was well-liked."

"It runs in the family."

She frowned at him, confusion on her face.

Nick tucked her hand into the crook of his arm and tugged her toward the door. "I meant, you're well-liked and your father was too."

"Oh."

She looked so lost. He said in a gentle voice, "You're tired."

"Not too tired." She gave him a weak smile, her meaning clear.

"I hope not." He needed tonight with her, to hold her and keep despair at bay.

They gathered Anjelita at the door. But a Latino man in his late twenties blocked their path. His face was ravaged by grief, his black hair unkempt, with dark circles under his eyes.

"Eddie!" Marisa said. "This is no place for you. Not so soon after Elizabeth."

So this was the husband of the woman floating in the Easterling's pond. No wonder he looked haggard.

"I had to come. My Elizabeth, she . . . " He sobbed, and then visibly rallied with a deep breath. "It was wrong, what we did, and she was taken from me because of it. I knew it was wrong to do."

Nick moved closer to Marisa. He didn't think he was going to like Eddie's confession.

"What did you do, Eddie?" Marisa asked.

"That Wentworth had to be stopped. I knew there'd be no buyer for the plant if there were trouble. So I made trouble." Eddie hung his head.

"Oh, Eddie."

"It was me. Elizabeth told me it wasn't right to make the plant lose money, even for a day. That's our honest labor at the plant. We work hard. But I was afraid. I heard the Chinese were going to make an offer. I couldn't think of anything else to do to stop that from happening. I asked Elizabeth to spy on Wentworth. I didn't know the storm would be that bad. So she drowned and it was all my fault. My gram says God punished me for doing something evil. I'm so sorry." He wept again.

Marisa laid her hand on his arm. "God didn't punish you, Eddie. It was a terrible accident. But you know the mayor and the sheriff want the name of who's behind the trouble at the plant. You should turn yourself in."

"I know. I had to tell you first, now that you own the plant." He swiped at his cheeks with a red handkerchief.

"That's not for sure yet."

"You're Easterling's daughter. No judge is going to give Easterling property to Wentworth instead of you."

Marisa didn't argue with him. "Have you got someone to go with you to the sheriff's office?"

He gave a slow shake of his head. "I got into this mess all by myself. I won't ask anyone else to be seen with me. Besides, with Elizabeth gone, I just don't care about anything anymore."

"She wouldn't want that, Eddie. She'd want you to pay the debt you owe and get back on track again."

"I can't think about her right now. It hurts too much." Eddie turned and walked away. His shoulders were hunched.

"Thanks for telling me, Eddie," Marisa said, her voice carrying.

"Did you want to go with him?" Nick asked.

"Yes, but he wouldn't appreciate it."

"He will need his family by him afterwards," her mother said.

Marisa looped her arm through her mother's. "I'll drive you home."

"How about if I drive you both?" Nick asked.

Marisa shook her head. "I need my car in the morning."

"Okay. I'll see you in a few minutes." He looked at Anjelita, who had a twinkle in her eye. Oh, what the hell. He kissed Marisa hard, a promise for later.

"I won't be long," she said.

*

Marisa walked her mother to the cottage door, but left the motor running.

"Do you love him, *mi hija*?"

"I don't know what I feel for him, but it's strong. Very strong. I wish I had more time with him."

"If he is the one, do not let him go."

"I held onto Kevin for eight years and look where that got me."

"The right man only comes into your life once."

"I've got to go, Mamá. I love you." Marisa kissed her mother's cheek.

"I love you too, *mi hija*. Do you forgive me for not telling you about your papa?"

"I'll get used to the idea eventually. Just give me a little time."

Her mother nodded and went inside the cottage. Marisa heard the lock click.

Marisa steered down the winding driveway. She was almost to the street when a blonde wraith appeared in her path, waving her arms. Marisa jammed on the brakes before she hit Scott's secretary. Her heart pounded hard in her chest. Brooke knocked on the passenger window and Marisa lowered it a little.

"I need to talk to you. There's something you need to know about Scott. Can I ride with you?" Her hair hung loose around her shoulders.

"What about Scott?" Had he murdered Carolyn? Was he behind the rash of accidents?

"We can't talk here. Please let me in."

Marisa unlocked the door and Brooke climbed in. The back door jerked open and Scott Wentworth slid into the car.

"Drive." Brooke pointed a gun at Marisa.

CHAPTER 18

Marisa stared at the gun Brooke held feeling stupid instead of terrified. Wasn't Scott the villain?

"Drive," Brooke said again, this time her voice deadly cold.

"Where?"

"Head north on Route 14 toward the wine country."

That made as much sense as Brooke pointing a gun at her, but when Brooke cocked it, Marisa put the car in gear and turned onto the street. She noticed Scott had disappeared from view and Brooke held the gun low where outsiders couldn't see it. So that's why his mistress was in the car. But it still didn't explain why she was the one holding the gun.

When Marisa reached Route 14, she glanced around. The harbor seemed deserted for the first time in her memory. She tried to think of some way to signal someone if she saw them. But any attention she brought to herself might get her and a potential rescuer shot. She wouldn't be the cause of someone else getting hurt.

"Don't try anything stupid," Brooke said. "Just drive."

So Marisa turned left onto 14. As she neared Salt Point Road, she thought about driving right up to Nick's cabin so he could help. He was a trained rescuer. But he was also unarmed. He'd suffered enough lately. She loved him enough not to want to add to his grief or to see him hurt.

Her breath caught. She gripped the wheel as she passed his road. She loved him. Of course she did. She empathized with him and cared whether his life held joy and beauty. She wanted to show him every beautiful place on the planet if it meant he would smile again.

Nick was everything she'd thought Kevin was—caring, dedicated, concerned, humanitarian, loving—but Nick was the real thing. How could she help but love him?

She had to make it back to him so she could tell him she loved him. She needed to think of how to outsmart these two. "I bet you think you got away with pushing Carolyn in front of the train."

"Shut up and drive," Brooke said.

"Aren't you afraid Scott's going to push you in front of a train?"

Brooke laughed. It wasn't a nice sound. "Scott and I have a partnership."

"What, you take turns killing people?"

"Something like that. After I went through Easterling's papers and found out you were his daughter, I knew you were a threat to Scott's inheritance."

Marisa jerked with surprise. Her father had documented her parentage? "So you wanted to prevent the DNA test? It's too late. People know I'm Easterling's daughter and next in line to inherit."

"I'm going to share Scott's wife's money, not you. You've proven to be a lot of trouble to us and I've had to expend a lot of effort trying to get rid of you."

Marisa felt battered by the shocks. "*You* were behind my accidents?"

Brooke's smile was smug. "No one suspected me. It worked beautifully. Well, almost. I thought that other woman was you. You always walk across the estate without looking to see who's following you. It was so perfect. People would think you drowned accidentally in the storm. I had a rude awakening when I found you at the door the next morning."

"So poor Elizabeth Hernandez died for nothing." Anger began to beat in her blood. Eddie was ravaged with guilt when the guilty party was right here in the car.

"I saw her at the window spying on us. Like I said, I thought it was you."

"Scott will be the first person they accuse if anything happens to me."

Brooke tsked. "You're overwrought. Everyone knows it. What with losing your fiancé, your best friend—who turned out to be your sister—and your apartment, not to mention finding out your parents were lying frauds, you're feeling pretty depressed. You're going to take a page from your sister and kill yourself."

Marisa tried to regulate her breathing. Her fingers ached from gripping the wheel. Her eyes ached from following the winding road in the dark after too many days with too little sleep.

"There's a flaw in your plan," Marisa said. "Deputy Nash doesn't believe Carolyn killed herself. Neither does his friend Nick Stark. Neither does my mother. The deputy already looked into Scott's business and found he needs cash. And he knows Scott lied about Carolyn seeing a shrink and taking antidepressants."

"What?" Scott sat up in the back seat. "That plan was foolproof. No small-town deputy should have doubted me. Who'd ever even think I pushed my wife to her death. She was always so boy bony it took no effort at all to make her lose her balance. I just can't believe I waited so long to do it."

Rage burned hot through Marisa's veins. Scott had killed Carolyn—her sister. He was a cold-blooded murderer. He had to pay for what he'd done. She wouldn't let him get away with it. "You didn't count on me."

"It doesn't matter," Brooke said. "You'll be out of the picture soon and we'll go back to the city with all that lovely Easterling money."

Lights pierced the night from the lakeside on Marisa's right as she passed the sign for the Showboat Motel & Restaurant. Marisa remembered they had a deep-water dock. Then she knew what she had to do. These two were going to kill her. She wasn't going to drive docilely to her death. She would make sure they paid for what they'd done to Carolyn and Elizabeth and her.

*

Marisa should have been here by now, Nick thought as he paced the cabin, his impatience an itch inside him he couldn't scratch. Doubt crowded in. Unless she'd changed her mind. Maybe she'd had time to think about seeing Kevin at the wake and had decided she didn't want to continue sleeping with Nick.

Had the sight of her ex-fiancé made her realize the shallowness of what she and Nick shared? Had she compared love to lust, and love won? If she could look into his heart, she'd see love there. If she'd just give him a chance, maybe she could love him like she'd loved her fiancé.

He looked out past the front porch again, but there was still no sign of her. He wanted this last night together, if that was all she'd give him.

Then it occurred to him that Marisa might not have changed her mind. Maybe she'd had car trouble—the man-made kind. God, he shouldn't have let her out of his sight. He should have followed her home.

He had to risk calling her mother's house, in case Marisa was there. But Anjelita told him Marisa had left there twenty minutes ago. The Easterling estate was only five minutes away by car. She should have been here by now. Something must have happened.

As he raced for his car, he called Brian on his cell phone. His friend answered on the first ring. "Marisa's missing! I'm getting into my car now and tracing a path from my house to her mother's."

"I'm at the Easterling house now to interview Wentworth's secretary. Nobody's home."

"Shit! He's got her!" Nick shifted the car into drive, spitting gravel from under the tires, and shot down the road.

"Don't panic, Nick. I'll put out an immediate APB on Scott's and Marisa's cars."

"If anything happens to her . . . " Nick couldn't finish. He didn't know how he'd be able to go on if she wasn't in the world. He gripped the steering wheel tighter.

"Don't think that way. I'm hanging up now to call in those APBs."

Nick prayed for the first time in a long time. He prayed to see Marisa again.

*

Marisa jerked the steering wheel to the right onto the Showboat's drive.

"Hey! Turn the car back." Brooke held the gun out toward Marisa.

Marisa didn't care. She had nothing to lose and everything to gain with her plan. She wasn't going to let a gun stop her and she didn't think Brooke would risk firing while Marisa was driving.

The car gained speed down the inclined driveway. She could see moonlight shimmering off the lake through a gap in the trees.

"Turn the car around," Scott said from the back seat.

But Marisa pushed the accelerator further to the floor. The car slewed around the curves. It sailed over the last hill landing with a whump that jarred her teeth.

In her peripheral vision, she was happy to see Brooke thrown against the door. Ha! There was a reason seatbelts were the law.

Scott gripped her seat. "What the hell are you doing? Stop this car at once!"

When hell freezes over, which was where she intended to send Scott and Brooke.

It was a clear, sloped path to Seneca Lake from here. She stomped the pedal to the metal. The car raced for the water.

"Jesus Christ! What are you doing?" Scott's voice was high with panic.

"Stop this car!" Brooke waved the gun at Marisa.

Die, bitch, Marisa thought at her.

"Omigod!" Scott shrieked as the front tires hit the wooden retaining wall.

Suddenly the car was airborne over the water. Marisa had a moment to savor the beauty of flying before she worked the electric window controls. As the front end of the car dipped toward the water, she locked the doors, turned off the engine and removed the key.

Brooke screamed. "You bitch!"

The impact was more jarring than Marisa had expected, and

with the windows cracked open and the driver's side completely down, the car sank a lot faster than she'd anticipated. Cold water flooded in. She released her seat belt and slid the seat all the way back. It all happened so slowly and that made her desperate. She didn't want to drown in this car. She had a lot to live for.

Working her way out of her seat, Marisa found it hard at first to push against the water.

Scott pummeled the car door. "Open the door!"

Marisa thanked God for childproof locks.

Brooke pushed against the door on her side. Marisa thought she'd get away free while they were occupied, but Brooke turned and seemed to realize Marisa was about to escape.

"Oh no you don't!" Brooke raised the gun and fired.

Marisa felt the burn against her arm as she ducked her head beneath the water, but it didn't stop her from pushing out through her open window and kicking free of the car. Nothing was going to stop her now. She swam in the direction she thought the surface was, kicking for all she was worth.

Before she expected it, her head broke the water's surface into air that felt chilled against her face. She gasped oxygen into her straining lungs. She was about 25 feet from shore. She marveled at how far the car had flown. She began a breaststroke to the retaining wall. Ahead of her, floodlights came on at the motel. A man ran across the lawn toward her.

Behind her she heard a splash. Damn! Marisa whirled and saw Brooke's pale hair and face reflected in the floodlight. If Brooke still had the gun, the people on the shore were in danger.

For a moment, Marisa was torn between trying to warn them and trying to eliminate Brooke's lethal threat. Protecting people seemed to have become second nature to her and she'd never have a better chance than now.

Marisa flung herself back toward Brooke. If she could catch the other woman by surprise . . . By the time Marisa reached her,

Brooke had raised the gun out of the water. It glinted in the light.

"Stop right there." Brooke didn't look so dangerous trying to stay afloat in the still disturbed water.

With all her strength, Marisa swung her arm up under Brooke's. The impact made the gun discharge, the loud blast echoing through the darkness. Marisa bobbed below the surface and when she kicked upward again she powered both her fists into Brooke's throat.

The other woman made strangled noises and then her eyes rolled up in her head. Her face sagged into the water. She deserved to drown.

Marisa sighed. Damn it, she'd have to save Brooke. She turned Brooke over so that she could grip the other woman around the neck. Slowly she paddled backwards to shore. Twenty-five feet had never seemed so long a distance.

When she was close enough she shouted, "Call 911."

"Already did!" a man shouted back.

Well, that was good. Marisa was feeling a little worn out from this hero business. She hoped she could see Nick soon and let him take over from here.

*

"What'd you find out?" Nick asked as Brian replaced the radio in his squad car.

"We just got a call. A car drove into the lake fifteen miles north of here."

Nick already had his car keys in his hand. "Jesus. Is it Marisa?"

"I don't know, but I'm heading up there now."

"I'm going too." Nick headed for his car at a run.

"The Showboat Motel & Restaurant. Watch for the sign. I'll lead the way."

Please God, let Marisa be all right, Nick prayed. He knew it had to be her, but he wondered what had happened. All the way there, as he drove at reckless speeds behind the strobing red and blue lights, his thoughts tortured him with what he might find when he arrived.

He skidded his car to a halt in the parking lot next to Brian's, jumped out and ran after his friend toward the lake. There was a line of people standing at the edge, and a ring of people around a woman's body on the ground.

A woman's body!

"Marisa!" He pushed the bystanders out of the way. "Marisa!" His brain couldn't make sense of what he was seeing—the woman was blonde. Brian dropped to his knees beside her.

"Nick."

Nick's head swiveled toward the voice. There stood Marisa with a blanket around her and her dark hair soaking wet. He nearly sagged with relief. He stumbled to her.

"Are you all right?"

"I am now." Her words came out through chattering teeth.

As though she was as breakable as spun glass, with wonder that she was alive and safe, he gathered her into his arms and sighed when she snuggled against him. "I was afraid I'd never see you again."

"Me too. When they told me to drive, I knew they didn't intend for me to come back."

He pulled far enough away to look into her face. "They?"

She nodded. "Scott and his secretary."

The blonde woman on the ground. He turned them so he could watch Brian work on Brooke. "What happened to her?"

Marisa lifted her chin. "I hit her in the throat."

Nick couldn't help the smile that broke free. "Good for you."

"She made me mad. She was the one who kept trying to kill me."

"No wonder Scott had an alibi. Where is he, by the way?" Nick looked around.

"In the car."

His gaze followed hers to the water. "In the car." He sounded as stupid as he felt.

"He killed Carolyn."

Now he understood. He looked at the water again and agreed with what she'd done. But, "Why didn't you try to get help? Why didn't you stop at my place instead of here?"

"I found I can be a hero too, Nick."

As more cops pulled into the parking lot with sirens blaring and lights strobing, he wondered where he'd heard that recently. He had the women he loved in his arms. He was content for the moment.

CHAPTER 19

The sky contained the first hints of sunrise by the time Marisa had had her gunshot wound stitched at the hospital, she'd satisfied her mother that she was fine, satisfied herself that Scott was truly dead and Brooke was in jail, and had given her statement to the police.

Marisa and Nick had escaped to his cabin to slake the desperate edge off their need for one another. Now she lay in his arms, soaking in the fire-hot heat of his flesh. Still, she couldn't seem to get warm enough. She pressed her lower body closer to his where their legs were tangled together.

"Give me a minute. That time nearly killed me." His voice sounded thick.

"You say that every time." She tried to joke; only she didn't feel like joking. This time with Nick was precious.

"I have to go home tomorrow," he said in a quiet voice.

Her happiness bubble burst. "I know." It was difficult to speak. She needed to tell him she loved him, but he was leaving and she didn't know how he felt about her.

"I wish I could stay, but as soon as I see the department shrink, I'll be cleared to go back to work."

"I know how important your job is to you."

"It is."

"Have you ever considered being an EMT someplace less . . . stressful?"

"Brian mentioned it to me. He said I could get a job almost anywhere in the country."

"You could go to California, learn how to surf." Marisa swallowed. She needed to know if he was another Kevin.

"I'm a New York boy. I don't think I'd be happy there. I like the seasons."

Marisa took a breath and plunged. "Do you think you could be happy here?"

Nick gripped her face between his hands. "Marisa, it's too soon for you. Less than a week ago you were preparing to marry another man."

"I know what I want, Nick, and that's you. I love you."

He hugged her tight. "You're mistaking desire for love."

Marisa pulled away from him, far enough to see his face was strained and serious once more. "I know what real love is now."

Nick shook his head. "We've hardly spent any normal time together. When we haven't been making love, we've been at the hospital, or fighting unknown villains, or fighting fire. That's not real life."

She opened her mouth to argue, but he placed a finger over her lips. "I bought another stimulator ring. Let's use it now."

Marisa kissed his finger and then moved it aside to kiss him hard. The fool. The sexy, warm, wonderful fool. What did it take to get through to him that she loved him when he'd lost hope that anything good would happen to him?

He swept his tongue into her mouth. She slipped a hand between their bodies to where his cock had hardened and stroked him. He groaned.

His hands found her sensitive nipples, stroking them to urgent tightness. She writhed against him, her breath coming in pants.

"How can I want you this badly?" He groaned, thrusting into her hands.

"It's only as badly as I want you. Please, Nick, fill me. Fill me hard and deep."

He growled and reached into the nightstand. Together they ripped open the packages and sheathed him with the condom and the vibrator ring. Then he entered her and to Marisa it felt like coming home.

Nick turned the vibrator on and began to ride her, pressing against her clitoris with each stroke. Marisa tried to hold back the tide, but Nick had taught her body to give in to the pleasure. The first orgasm crested fast.

She helped Nick pull her legs high up his back so that he applied constant stimulation to her clitoris. She rode him, accepting his deep thrusts, wanting to take him fully into her body and become one with him.

As the minutes wore on, he seemed to catch her desperation. He drove deeper, harder, almost violently.

"Come on. Give me everything, Marisa."

She tried. She raised her hips to his. He folded her body practically in half, seeming driven by her cries to seal himself to her.

But they were still separate. She wanted no division from him. "Make me yours."

Nick rolled her over. Repositioning her on her knees, he became a wild man. His thrusts were urgent. "Mine. Mine. Mine." He chanted to his thrusts.

No sooner had the vibrator ceased, than Nick thrust hard and came with a hoarse shout. For a moment, she felt the unity she desired. But it lasted only a moment.

Marisa dropped her head to the bed, panting. Behind her, Nick's breaths sawed in and out.

As he withdrew, wetness slid down her inner thigh.

Nick groaned. "Shit." She knew what had happened before he told her. "The condom broke."

It was as though fate had intervened, but she wouldn't be ruled by fate. She rolled over to face him.

For a moment, his expression looked pained. Then it firmed with resolve. "I'll marry you if you're pregnant."

It was not the words she wanted to hear, not when she wanted a profession of love. "I wouldn't do that to you."

"I know my duty, Marisa. I won't do to you what your father did to your mother."

"I don't need to be rescued, Nick, and you don't have to sacrifice yourself for me. I love you too much for that."

"You don't love me. You're still in love with Kevin."

"No, I'm not." She shook her head. "Kevin was puppy love, a high school crush. You . . . you're the only man for me."

"You don't know what you're saying."

Marisa sat up. "I'm saying I want to make you happy. I want to see you smile every day. I want to wake up to you making coffee, and I want to go to bed every night so sated by your lovemaking that I don't hear thunderstorms. I want to make love to you every fall at Eagle Cliff Falls with the cold water and your heated flesh. I want to walk the gorge with you and watch you go off fishing with Brian on weekends. I want to have children with you."

The reminder of children brought pain to his eyes. She tried to chase it away. "But not if it means trapping you where you don't want to be. I want a partner, not a savior." She read in his eyes that he wanted what she offered, but he couldn't believe it.

If you love something, set it free, so she did. "You can go home if you want to, Nick. Go home to the stress of a joyless life. Or you can stay here with me. I don't want you to go, but I won't hold you here. If you need time," she swallowed, "take all the time you need. I'll be here waiting."

Nick cupped her face in his hands. "I love you so much."

Marisa's heart soared with hope.

"Are you sure?" he asked. "I need you to be sure."

"I've never been surer."

"Then I don't need more time, at least not time to decide. But I'd like another fifty or sixty years with you."

Marisa hugged him. It felt good to be able to rescue him.

EPILOGUE

"Look what I found." Marisa waved the book at Nick. "It's Carolyn's diary. It was hidden in my father's," she tripped over the not-yet-familiar word, "desk. Scott or Brooke must have taken it out of the box of mementos." Sorrow crossed her heart, like a cloud passing over the sun. They hadn't taken the box out of her trunk, so most of the photos in the box had been ruined in the lake water, although a local photographer said he'd try to save them.

Nick pulled her down onto the couch next to him, wrapped an arm around her and kissed her cheek. "Try not to think about what you've lost. We own the Easterling house, the salt plant is saved, and we're getting married tomorrow."

"And your brother's coming to be your best man."

Nick had contacted his brother to let him know he was moving to Watkins Glen. He'd found out his brother didn't blame him for their father's death. It had been Nick's own guilt that had caused the rift between them.

"We have a lot to be thankful for." Marisa snuggled against him. She turned to the last page on which anything was written. She glanced at it, and then looked harder. Then she sat up straight and grabbed Nick's arm. "Nick, listen to this."

"To my sister Marisa. Yes, it's true—we're sisters. I found out from my father's papers after he died. He hadn't wanted to hurt my mother by claiming you while she was alive, but he was planning to claim you publicly for your thirtieth birthday. He'd meant for us to share his inheritance.

"I'd known since I was a teenager that my father and your mother were sleeping together. I'd thought it was an affair. But then I found my dad's papers and understood your parents had been lovers since I was born. I found the wedding rings with the vows he'd written for

170

their wedding. Had my mother died, they would have married. That's when I knew it was more than an affair—your mother was the wife my mother could no longer be.

"If something happens to me, I've left your parents' wedding rings for you to give to your mother. It's time she admitted she was also Mrs. Easterling. And you're an Easterling too.

"I've put up with Scott's philandering because I thought my mother put up with my father's affair. But once I found out the truth about your parents, I realized my mother had to have known your mother was like his other wife. He was devoted to both of them. I know I can't tolerate Scott's behavior anymore. I'm leaving him I know I'll probably never find anyone to love me like my father loved your mother, but I'm going to try. I deserve it.

"I wish I could tell you this instead of writing it. I don't know why your mother continues to keep her secrets. Maybe she doesn't want to hurt me. But I'm not hurt, Marisa. I'm ecstatic to know the truth, about them and about us.

"I love you more now that I know we're related. I hope we'll get to share the truth soon.

"Love, Caro."

Marisa sniffed and rubbed tears from her cheeks.

Nick kissed her forehead. "Now you know all the truth."

"The truth is more important than the facts." — *Frank Lloyd Wright*

ABOUT THE AUTHOR

Shay Lacy writes stories about love that transforms. You can see all of her novels on her website, *www.shaylacy.com*. You can find her on Facebook and Twitter. You might also find her in beautiful places around the United States and Canada with either a pen or a camera in hand, sometimes both. Shay loves to hear from readers. You can e-mail her at: *shay_lacy@yahoo.com.*

In the mood for more Crimson Romance? Check out *Nature of the Beast* by Stephanie Freeman at *CrimsonRomance.com*.

www.ingramcontent.com/pod-product-compliance
Lightning Source LLC
Chambersburg PA
CBHW010639100726
47900CB00011B/2899